A Motherless Child

by

KATRINA WADE

A Motherless Child
Copyright © 2022 by Katrina Wade

ISBN
978-1-958690-74-1 (Paperback)
978-1-958690-75-8 (eBook)

KATRINA WADE

A Motherless Child

Dedication

Ora Lee Wade 1945-1976 Mama

David Porter Sprawls 1944-2013 Daddy

I dedicate this book to my Amazing children Kye, Tia, Steven, and Danielle, who has kept me sane and gave me a purpose for living, because of them I could not let the sorrow or pain of my childhood dictate my life, these four individuals and I use that word loosely as they are their unique person, they have all played an important role in molding me into the woman that I am today.

Love you guys always & forever

ACKNOWLEDGMENTS

First and foremost, I'd like to give honor to Jesus Christ my Lord and Savior who is first in my life, I thank him for always keeping me and never forsaking me, he is now and has always been my help in times of trouble, at a young age I knew to look to him for comfort. I thank him for his grace and mercy every day anew, for all that I've endured, the strength to go thru it, and the victory of coming out unscathed, whole and complete.

To God be the glory

I'd like to thank the little girl that still lives inside of me for being so strong and courageous, because of her nothing gets the best of me or keeps me down, she is my courage, and her plight motivates me and helps me to keep moving forward.

Don't ever leave me

I'd like to thank my sisters who gave me a vision of whom our Mother was, Due to circumstances beyond our control we never got the opportunity to really get to know each other or get to live as sisters, but the love that we have for one another is real, just like Mommy taught us.

Love, Love, Love you all to life

To all of my girlfriends, there are so many of you, too many to name, some of you have come and gone, it's true when they say some people come into your life for a season, and to those that are still around, I'd like to thank you for standing in the gap and being my sisters when I needed you the most.

You all may not have known just what you all have contributed to my life, but every one of you has made a deposit into my heart and has been exactly what I have needed at the exact moment. How many of you know that it wasn't by coincidence? That our paths crossed but by divine intervention.

Thank you for being my sister- friends.

Much Love.

And lastly to Mr. Leonard McGee, my longtime platonic friend, who has served as a brother, an uncle, and a father figure to both me and my children. I know that God has placed you in our lives and in my heart, you are the brother that I never had; I love you more than you will ever know. I sincerely thank you for always being there for us, I'm grateful to have you in my life.

XOXOXO

TABLE OF CONTENTS

Acknowledgments vii

Introduction xv

Chapter 1   The Beginning of The End – Mama.................................... 1

Chapter 2   Beauty School 4

Chapter 3   The Fight..7

Chapter 4   Mama 10

Chapter 5   The Talk 13

Chapter 6   The Premonition –Shelia 15

Chapter 7   Grandma & Big Mama.. 18

Chapter 8   Saying Goodbye 21

Chapter 9   The Beatings 25

Chapter 10   Queenie 28

Chapter 11   The Funeral 30

Chapter 12   The Stabbing 34

Chapter 13   The Insurance Policy 39

Chapter 14   Garbage Picker 42

Chapter 15   The Almost Drowning.................................... 44

Chapter 16   Uncle 47

Chapter 17   The Truancy Officer 49

Chapter 18   The Letter..51

Chapter 19   Charlene Comes Home 54

Chapter 20   Thanksgiving... 56

Chapter 21   The Court House 58

Chapter 22   The Wait 60

Chapter 23   Boxing Ring 62

Chapter 24   Weekend Visit With Daddy 65

Chapter 25   Sunday... 68

Chapter 26   The Police..74

Chapter 27   The Social Worker 76

Chapter 28   The Pink Huffy 81

Chapter 29   The Disappearing Bike 84

Chapter 30   The Confrontation...................................... 88

Chapter 31   The Fight.. 92

Chapter 32   She Had Enough 95

Chapter 33   Going Home With Daddy............................ 98

A MOTHERLESS CHILD

The beginning of the end - Mama

Get up, get up, banging on the front door, Ebony, Ebony Y'all get up and open this door was all that I heard, Ebony got down from the top bunk and went to the door, who is it? She said as she opened the door, what's going on? What are you all doing here? Where is mama? As she fired off one question after the last. No one is answering any of her questions. They all come into the house and immediately start rummaging thru things, Ebony says mama is gonna be mad if Y'all mess up her house. Girl yo mama is dead! Someone said, Ebony screamed Wait, What Did you say? Monee came running out of the room and said our mama is dead? She started crying, why, what happened? Shelia just sat in her bed staring thru the door of the bedroom, I said Shelia, what did they say about mama, Shelia said just come here missy, get in the bed with me, we sat there and watched as they rummaged thru our mother's things, taking everything that wasn't nailed down, we just sat there and watched as our sisters tried to stop them.

INTRODUCTION

This is a story of A little girl who was lost and alone, she is one of four sisters whose lives will be forever changed. The eldest is Ebony (14) then Monica aka Monee (12), Shelia (10), and Katrina (5) Katrina was the baby of the group, the last of the four girls. I Katrina the girl who never belonged. The motherless child.

CHAPTER 1

The Beginning of
The End – Mama

Mama's frying chicken, Ike &Tina Turner's Proud Mary is blaring in the background, Ebony, Monee, and Shelia are sitting at the table dying Easter eggs, tomorrow would be Easter day, and the girls are excited to open their baskets filled with toys and candy, they are more excited to wear their new dresses to church, and I'm sitting watching, they say that I'm too young to help, although I know that I'm not.

Knock, knock there was a knock at the door, mama went to the door, who is it she asked, it's me, Charlene & Mary, Gene, and Lois just pulled up too, mama open the door and said hey y'all, what are y'all doing here this evening, Charlene and Mary were mamas, sisters, Gene and Lois were mama's friends they worked together, we all called Lois Aunt, she and mama were very close friends, I never understood why we would call mama's friend aunt when we didn't call her sisters aunt. Mama was the oldest of the girls but came from a family of nine, Charlene was next and Mary the baby of the girls, we all loved Mary she had such a bubbly personality, but Charlene not so much, it was something about her that just didn't feel right she never seemed to be happy, she seemed to always find a problem in every situation.

Mama said come on in, what brings y'all over here tonight? Charlene said I came to get my hair done, mama threw her head back and said I thought that you were coming by the shop today? Charlene said I got tied up, mama said umm-hmm shaking her head as she laughed it off, they all laughed, Charlene said y'all know how it is as she made a funny face while she laughed. Mama said ok after I finish cooking and feeding the kids, I'll do your hair, what's in the bag? We stopped at the liquor store, and we picked up some whiskey and some beer said Mary, oh, ok I'll get some glasses mama said as they walked into the kitchen, just then Gene said girl you're jamming in here, and that chicken is calling my name, Mama laughed and said well hello to you too greedy, Gene said while he was laughing hey girl, you know that I love to eat me some fried, chicken, especially your fried chicken, can nobody fry chicken like you girl, whatever Gene you don't have to gas me up, mama said, what are you cooking with it? Gene asked, Mama, said rice, corn, and a piece of white bread; with some hot sauce on the side, as she snaps her fingers, he said do you have enough for me Mama said absolutely. I shouted to Gene and ran to him, he picked me up saying hey my pretty brown girl, I loved the attention from him plus he always brought me candy, but I had to ask, did you bring me candy? You know that I did, I have some for all of my girls he answered, Can I have it now mama? Mama said No, Gene you know that baby needs to have dinner first, he said alright Ora; but missy when you're done we're gonna eat us a Reese's, cup, can I have a whole one by myself? I asked, Yes you can he said but after you eat ok? I said shook my head as to say yes, as he put me down, Mama said Trina use your words and I said yes Sir. Mama said I thought y'all said that Lois was pulling up too, Gene said she is, let me go see if she's ok, just then Aunt Lois said Ladies where y'all at, were in the kitchen Mama said, Hey girl Lois said as she made her way thru the kitchen door, Mama got up went over to hug her, she said it must be a full moon, you out here tonight and all, Lois said no I was on my way home and stopped by her to borrow your green shoes, I wanna wear them to church tomorrow, Mama said ok yea, I remember you asked me that earlier in the week, they are in my closet, grab them on your way out, Charlene and Mary brought some drinks you want a glass? Lois says yall got some CC, Mary said of course as they both laughed.

The girls were just finishing up dying the eggs; mama said Ebony y'all get the table cleaned off and go in the living room I'll call y'all when dinner is ready. Ok, mama, and she did what she was told, we all left the kitchen.

Ebony and Monee were in the living room talking, Ebony says ooohweee, I don't like Charlene, I don't know why Mama can't see it, Monee says I know, do you see how she looks at mama? I swear that she is just jealous of her, Her and grandma, I've never known a mother to be jealous of her own child Ebony said, then Monee added and I don't care for her much either she's just mean for no reason, I hate it when mama leave us over there, Ebony said I know me too, do you remember that time we were in the car and we were telling mama how mean grandma was to us when she left us over there for the week when she went to that stupid hair show? Monee said yea, then mama started yelling at us, but she started crying but wouldn't tell us what was wrong. What was that about? Ebony said yes I remember, poor mama she is so sad, I wonder what happened to her. I don't know but it was something because she is always talking to us about being all that we have, I don't even know what that means, I know said Monee, but when I get grown I'm gonna take mama away from this socalled family. Just then Mama called Ebony to come on and fix the plates.

CHAPTER 2

Beauty School

Mama was a hairdresser, she had a natural talent for growing hair, and she owned a small salon with just three booths she was very proud of herself. Mama came from a single-parent home and life was hard, they were poor and most of her upbringing was dysfunctional at best, she was raised in rural Mississippi and during those times it was what it was, Mama thrived to have a better life, she just knew that life was more than what she was living. She was the oldest girl, she had to help her Mother out with the other girls she would always do their hair for school and over the years she just became the miracle worker of hair, she branched out and started doing friends' hair for a few dollars, sometimes she would barter for things such as shoes and clothes before long her Saturdays were filled with doing hair, she really enjoyed doing it plus the little money often helped her mom to support the family. When mama was 18 years old one of her cousins that lived in Chicago Illinois had come to visit, she was telling Mama about the beauty school that had just opened not far from where she lived, and how she could enroll there, that way she could get professionally trained. Mama was excited about it; she decided that she was going to do it. the day before her cousin was due to leave and head back home to Chicago, she went onto the back porch where her mother was sitting shelling peas, she said Mama I'm leaving to go back to Chicago with Merle. Merle says that there is a beauty school that's not far from her house that I could go to so that I can get trained professionally to do hair, her Mother just sat there she didn't respond, Mama-said Merle said that I could stay at the house with her parents and her, and when I get done I can get a job and send you money to help out, her mother just sat there still shelling the peas as if she didn't hear mama talking to her, Mama said and when I save up enough money I can send for yall and things will be better, her mother still didn't respond, Mama then said I'm sorry mama but I just want a better life and want to be able to help you, as if that last statement had been a bolt of lightning her Mother jumped up from the chair, the bowl of peas that she had been shelling fell to the porch and the peas scattered and rolled away, she said I don't need your damn help I always knew that you thought that you were better than me, I tell you what Ms. Fancy hair dresser, you don't have to wait till they leave you get your rags and get out of my god damn house now, hell I don't need you for nothing.

Mama just stood there as the tears started to run down her face she said Mama I wasn't saying that, I just want us to, before she could get another word out of her mouth, her mother slapped her in the face yelling get out, get out with your ungrateful black ass, all that I've done for you, you have a lot of nerve, get out now and don't ever think about coming back, when you get out there and fall on your natural black ass you can't come crawling back to me, you thank cuss you know how to hot comb some hair that's gonna be good enough to go to some hair school? Mama tried to answer her, but her mother slapped her again and then said get out now!!, mama just walked off the porch, she had nowhere to go she was just walking and crying.

Ora, Ora she heard her cousin Merle calling her name as she ran to catch up with Mama, she said Ora what happened Cousin Piggy is going off? Mama's Mother's Nickname was piggy, that's what family and some friends called her.

Mama just said you know how she is, I can never do anything right for her, no matter what I do, I'm just tired of being abused, Merle said that's ok, my dad told me to come to get you, mama said I'm not going back because I don't want to be disrespectful to my Mother and how I'm feeling right now if she hits me again I might hit her back, Merle said I understand, well I'm gonna go get your stuff, Mama chuckled and said she ain't gonna let you get nothing for me, Merle said she's like that? mama said oh you have no idea, but she is still my Mother, Merle said if she doesn't we can share my clothes, I don't have much but we gotta do what we gotta do and she hugged mama and mama began to cry again.

Merle said just to stay here I'm going back to the house to see what's going on, Mama went to sit under a tree, and she began to pray, God please help me, I have had enough, please let my Mother be ok but I have to go, I love her but I have to go, and god please let her love me one day, and let her understand that I'm just trying to help, help us all to have a better life.

Thank you, Amen.

CHAPTER 3

The Fight

We all went into the kitchen, mama had gotten out the straitening comb to press out Charlene's hair, Ebony made the plates, and we all sat down to eat only I played around with my food with the spoon, I didn't want to eat I just wanted the candy, it was all that I could think about. Shelia said Missy you better eat, I said I don't want it, Shelia said you know that mama ain't gonna let you get up until your done and I'm not eating it for you tonight, I said I don't want it, mama said well get up from there, your little butt is gonna be hungry. Mama, can I have my candy now? She just looked at me and said Gene you done got her all excited about that candy, go on and give it to her, Yaaaaa I shouted as I jumped down from the table and ran over to Gene who was sitting near the back door, the girls finished eating and went into their room. Mama and her guest all sat around drinking and smoking cigarettes while mama did Charlene's hair. About an hour or so later, I walked into the kitchen and said mama I want chicken now, Mama called to Ebony, come get Missy some chicken, Mama was doing Mary's hair now, Ebony walked into the kitchen says yes Ma'am, and proceeded to fix the plate of food. I said I don't want any food just chicken, as I was jumping up and down, Ebony says ok Missy as if she was aggravated with me.

Charlene said that girl is too damned spoiled, Mama responded leave my baby alone ain't nothing wrong with spoiling your kids. Charlene didn't like the fact that I could get whatever I wanted from mama and the girls so she always had something to say about what was going on with me. I sat down at the table and ate the chicken, Charlene sat there and watched me the entire time, I said mama I want another chicken, Charlene said to eat all of that meat off that bone, just wasting food, Mama said Charlene it's ok I brought the damn chicken, Charlene said you ought to make her sit down and eat, she can't get full on meat alone, Mama said Aww girl let that baby alone, she's alright and before mama could get the chicken for me, Charlene reached over to the stove and snatched the last piece of chicken and threw it to the dog, I began screaming and crying that made mama mad, she shouted Charlene why would you do that when you heard my baby saying that she wanted some more? Now you have gone too damn far, you need to get yourself together because you're pissing me off now, you always have something to say about how I'm raising my kids and I'm sick of it, these are my damn kids and I can raise them how I damn well please, you need to go and have you some kids. I don't want any kids Charlene yelled back, and you don't have to worry about me saying nothing else to you or your damn kids! come on Mary lets go before I get mad up in here, and kick somebody's ass, Mama said I don't care, get mad you know that you were wrong, I'm telling you girl you had better mind your business when it comes to me and my kids. And I can promise you that you won't be kicking my ass.

Just then Charlene jumped up from the table and grabbed a beer bottle and threw it at Mama, the bottle hit the refrigerator and shattered and glass went flying throughout the kitchen, then Charlene ran towards mama and the two of them were fighting, Ebony grabbed me and we ran out of the kitchen, we stood and watched as they were fighting and tearing up the kitchen, Monica and Shelia ran into the doorway where we were standing to watch them fighting also, Sheila and I were crying, our dog Queenie who will later be my savior was barking and growling uncontrollably, before running over to the fighting women she began biting at Charlene's pant leg, it was just chaos, everyone was yelling and trying to break up the fight, I was so afraid I had never seen anything like it. But that would become the norm in my life. Gene was able to pull the two apart, Charlene shouted Ora I'm gonna get you, mark my word, I'm gonna get your black ass, then she knocked everything down from the counter before she walked out. Mary was crying and saying I'm sorry as she was running out of the door behind Charlene, Ebony closed and locked the door.

Mama came over and picked me up she kissed me and said mama is ok, don't cry, she walked to the bathroom and my sisters followed her, as she put me down on the toilet, she looked in the mirror checking her face for bruises and started talking to us, she said girl's mama is so sorry that you all had to see that, I really didn't mean for that to happen, I had no choice but to defend myself. We have always had a strange relationship, Charlene can be so mean and nasty at times, she has always been that way, but I still love her because she is my sister, Mama grabbed a towel from the towel rack wet it, and wiped her face, wiping away her tears, she says what she and I just did, I don't ever want to see you girls doing that, it will break my heart, love one another because you're all that you have in this world. My Mother didn't teach us how to love each other and we have always fought, violence was the way that we were taught to settle things and that's WRONG!!!, that's why I'm always talking to you girls, teaching you how to love one another, I felt like it was my job to stop the cycle. Do you understand? we all said yes.

CHAPTER 4

Mama

Mama put on a pot of coffee while she, Aunt Lois, and Gene cleaned the kitchen, mama sat at the table and lit a cigarette, she had such a sad look on her face. Lois said Girl, are you ok? that thang is just plum crazy, talking about Charlene, they all laughed, and she said Ora you ought to quit fooling with her, I know that she is your sister but she is too quick to put her hands on you, girl you don't need nobody else trying to beat on you, you've been thru enough, mama sat there looking right thru Aunt Lois, girl, do you hear me? Aunt Lois said as Mama just sat there. Gene said she is right Ora think about it, sometimes you gotta love folks from a distance. You can do it, you left that husband for putting his hands on you, hell you quit fooling around with Trina's daddy who stayed jumping on you too, you can quit fooling with Charlene too, Mama said that's different, those were just men and they come a dime a dozen, Charlene is my sister, I just think that one day were gonna get it right, Gene says that's very honorable of you Ora, it is, it really is but at what point will enough be enough? Aunt Lois says that's true, I mean she is fighting you bout what you're letting your child eat in your own damn house, hell the food that you brought, that makes no sense to me, mama said I know but I love her and things will get better just you all wait and see, they have too I've been praying and asking Jesus to fix this family, lawd knows he is the only one that can.

Gene scratches his head in disbelief he says Ora your just a peacemaker always seeing the good in people but baby you need to see people for who they are, as he throws his hands up in the air, I'm gonna get outta here you call me if you need me, cheer up sis, I love you girl, mama got up and hugged him she says I love you too bro, as she walked Gene to the door. As Mama walked back into the kitchen Lois said I made you a cup of coffee sit down let me talk to you, Ora you know that I love you like you were my sister, right? Mama said yes, I do know that, I want you to take what I'm about to say to you in love, ok? Yes Lois mama said with an exasperated voice, how much longer are you going keep going thru this with Charlene, you told me that you were done the last time you all fell out, you should have been done when she jumped on you when Trina was a baby, hell you were holding her in your arms, she wasn't even a week old and you accidentally dropped her, your body wasn't even healed and that girl kicked you all up in your stomach, she can't love you, don't you know that when you have children that your life is not your own anymore, that everything that you do going forward is for the benefit of them, I know Lois mama interrupted and said but you don't understand, they are all that I have, I love my family and that's how we love I guess, that's all that we know, for as long as I can remember we've been fighting each other, Mostly us fighting with Charlene, Mary and I have never fought, the two of us are always fighting with Charlene. Lois interrupted it doesn't matter who you're fighting with the point that I'm trying to make is that it's not normal and what kind of example are you setting for your daughters? Do you want them behaving like this, of course not Mama answered, no not at all, but what can I do? I have to defend myself. Lois said you wouldn't have to defend yourself if you didn't have her around, she is gonna end up killing you, Mama said now Lois that's low even for Charlene, I don't think that she will go that far, Lois stated shaking her head and said Hmmm, it's obvious that she cares nothing for you, she fights to kill each time, but then turns right around and says that she loves you, ORA, WAKE UP AND SMELL THE COFFEE!!, that's not love by any means, you are a grown woman you can do what you want but as a friend and someone who truly loves you, girl I'm telling you this isn't normal, I'm sorry for raising my voice and I'm done talking about it but you had better take heed, you are all that these girls have what would happen to them if something was to happen to you? Mama said your right Lois I know but I can't turn my back on my sisters, my love won't let me do that, I've never thought about what would happen to my girls if something happened to me, they have good fathers who both come from good families, I'm sure that one of them would take my girls and raise them. But I'm not gonna start with that stinking thinking, I'm gonna raise my girls, god wouldn't have given them to me if I wasn't supposed to raise them, I believe that Lois I hear you and I appreciate you and I understand what you're saying I do, I just got to figure out how to make this relationship with my sister better.

CHAPTER 5

The Talk

I had been standing in the hallway listening to that entire conversation, at five years old I didn't have a real concept of what was being said so I decided to go to Ebony, I asked her why Charlene had fought mama when I was just a week old? And if I was hurt when mama dropped me, Ebony said who told you that? I heard Aunt Lois say that to Mama, well when you were a baby Mama and Charlene got into a fight about something and everyone was breaking up the fight, mama was feeding you when Charlene grabbed mama's hair from the back and started hitting her in the face, mama accidentally dropped you, she jumped up and started fighting back, after they broke up the fight mama called the police and ambulance came to take you to the hospital, I'm not sure what happened next but you had to stay there for two days. Why did she do that I asked. Ebony said because she is nuts. Just then Mama and Aunt Lois walked up, mama said girls come to say goodnight to Aunt Lois, and we all went to give her a hug and a kiss, I'll see you all at church in the morning, love you girls, Aunt Lois said, we all said, I love you, oh wait girl I'm forgetting what I came over here for Lois said, Mama said I just bout forgot too, go on in my room to get them, they are on the shoe rack inside the closet door, Lois went to get the shoes, mama walked Aunt Lois to her car.

We were in our room, which was the dining room turned into a bedroom, mama couldn't afford a 2-bedroom apartment, so the room didn't have an actual door just an archway. Mama stood at the entrance to our bedroom, where we had two sets of bunkbeds a toy chest, two Chester of drawers, and a TV on a stand, she told us how much she loved us and that she would do anything to protect us, she said come here girls and she tried to hug all four of us at once. She apologized to us and said that we would never have to see her fighting again, mama said the next time that I see Charlene I'm going to talk to her, were gonna stop all of this arguing and fighting it's not healthy, we're gonna have a real woman to woman talk, gonna find out why we can't get along. Then she paused and held her head down for a moment, when she lifted her head up, her eyes were filling up with tears, she said But Ebony you're the oldest, and if anything, ever happens to me, you help take care of your sisters as best as you can, and you tell them that I don't want y'all to be separated Ebony said mama why are you saying that? Mama says I'm just saying if anything ever does I want y'all to stay together, Ebony said mama don't talk like that, mama said I'm sorry love, I'm not trying to scare you, but sometimes you just talk about hard things, do you understand? she looked so sad but she tried to act as if was everything was ok, she clapped her hands if that would lighten the mood and started talking about Easter Dinner, what she had planned to cook, who we were going to visit after church and at that moment, it felt like everything was back to normal.

CHAPTER 6

The Premonition
–Shelia

Later on, that night we all were watching TV, and trying to have a normal evening, when there was a knock on the door, before Mama could answer the door, Shelia yelled mama don't answer the door, everyone was surprised because Shelia never really spoke much and especially not a yell, Mama said awe baby it's gonna be alright, as she went to answer the door. Who is it mama asked. it's me, Charlene, mama opened the door, it was Charlene and Mary, Charlene said I'm sorry Sister, I just had too much to drink, mama hugged her and said I know that's right, and sadly enough just seeing them seem to perk her up, Mama loved her family and genuinely wanted a relationship with them. Mama invited them in, and we all sat on the sofa watching them as they came thru the door, Ebony and Monee looked at each other and rolled their eyes, they just did not like it when Charlene came over, Ebony said ohh she is so fake, Monee didn't respond, Mama seemed like she was happy that they were there she says what's in those bags? As she laughed, and they all laughed Charlene said I brought us matching outfits, I wanna go out tonight as they walked towards the kitchen, the kitchen in our house was the meeting place, whenever anyone came over they always ended up in the kitchen, mama really didn't like people sitting on her furniture, furniture was made to last a lifetime back in those days. Shelia just stood there frozen in time with a look of despair on her face, Ebony and Monee tried to get her to tell them what was bothering her, but all she said was we ain't never gonna see mama again., she just stood there and said it over and over again.

Shelia was always a peculiar child, just a bit more standoffish than the other girls, quiet and unassuming; she was very observant and saw everything. Ebony said girl what is wrong with you? as Shelia stood there staring into space, Monee went to get mama, Mama walked into the living room and said Shelia Baby what's bothering you? The words jumped out of Sheila's mouth Mama don't go with them, we ain't never gonna see you again if you do, Mama said ain't nothing gonna happen to Mama, I know that you're scared because you saw us fighting earlier, sometimes sisters fight baby, I already explained that to you remember, but I don't ever wanna see you all fighting each other, love one another because you all are all that you have, and you all have to stick together and always get along ok? Yes Ma'am we all said in Unison. Now I don't want to hear any more of that crazy talk, go on in there and brush your teeth and get ready for bed. Shelia just stood there and watched Mama walk away. Sheila walked towards the kitchen, she stood at the kitchen door and said please don't hurt our Mama, Mary said what? Sheila, what are you talking about? Before Shelia could answer Mama yelled at her GO TO BED NOW!

Charlene just sat there as if she knew exactly what Sheila was talking about, Mama tried to explain that Sheila was just scared because of what she had seen earlier, and that she was concerned, that it wasn't a big deal, she says you know kids are people too, and they have the same feelings as us adults as if she needed to explain to them why her child had said what she said. Mary said I'm sorry that we brought that mess to your house, Charlene said look I don't want to be talking about that shit all night,

They all just stood there in awkward silence for a few minutes, Mama broke the ice by saying let me see what's in these bags, Ooh Wee girl, this looks good, Mama said while checking out the outfits that Charlene brought, brought them all matching outfits, A black long sleeved leotard, and a pair of dark washed bell bottom jeans, mama said I hope that you got the right size, you know I was blessed with these hips and she laughed,

Charlene rolled her eyes and said you are so full of yourself, Mama said girl whatever you see these hips as she was rubbing her hands over her hips, looking around and neither of her sisters appreciated that gesture, so mama said while rolling her eyes, anyway these are nice and I have the perfect pair of wedges to wear with them. Mary said I'm wearing these as she pulled out a pair of black booties, Mama said where are we going? down to Woods Mary replied. Woods was the neighborhood dive bar that they usually frequented, everybody knew everybody there, it was nothing special the drinks were strong and cheap and the music was good and loud, they always had a good time.

Let's get dressed before it gets too late and we can't find a seat Mary said. Shelia who was still standing at the doorway began to follow mama around saying please don't go, don't leave us, mama, we're never gonna see you again, Mama turned around and yelled at Shelia saying WHAT DID I JUST SAY TO YOU? I DON'T WANT TO HEAR ANYMORE OF THIS FOOLISHNESS NOW GO TO BED! DO YOU UNDERSTAND ME?! Shelia walked away turned to look at Mary and Charlene and said please don't take our mama away from us, mama yelled SHELIA MARIE WARE, YOU ARE ASKING FOR IT! AND I'M FIVE MINUTES AWAY FROM GIVING IT TO YOU!! Shelia walked into the bedroom and climbed on her bed, and just stared at the ceiling. Something was bothering that girl, she just didn't know to explain it to her mother, but she knew that it was serious.

The three sisters continued getting dressed, laughing, drinking, and dancing like they hadn't a care in the world. Mama came into the bedroom and said goodnight ladybugs, I'm going out for a little while, turn the TV off and go to bed, I love you guys more than you will ever know, we all except Shelia said goodnight mama, we love you too, they walked out of the door, Shelia sat up in the bed and said that's it, we will never see her again. Ebony said stop it, Sheila, your creeping me out, Monee chimed in yea that's pretty creepy Shelia. And then there was silence.

CHAPTER 7

Grandma & Big Mama

Our grandma walked in while everyone was still rummaging, the first thing that she said was Ebony where is your Mothers insurance policy? Ebony said I want to know what's going on, what happened to my mama. Grandma, why are they taking our stuff? The poor girl was screaming to the top of her lungs wanting to be heard. Grandma yelled girl shut your damn fast ass mouth, where is the god damn policy, Ebony said I don't know, come on Monee and they walked into the bedroom and joined Shelia and me, we just sat there confused, it seemed like hours had passed as we sat there hoping that someone would tell us something when grandma came to the door of our bedroom and said Ebony grab yall some clothes, I'm gonna have to take y'all's asses to my house, I sho don't want to be bothered with no mo damn kids, Ebony do you know yo daddy's phone number? Ebony said yes, call him then grandma said, Ebony called and reached her grandmother, her father's mother who said that she was on her way over. And the drama begins!

Big Mama is what the girls called their grandma, they really loved her and she loved all of us, she wouldn't just do for them, she did for me as well, although I wasn't her biological granddaughter she still accepted me as if I were, she and Mama had a good relationship she often babysat all of us, she helped Mama out by buying groceries, helping with shoes and clothes whatever she could do to help, I liked her a lot.

When Big mama showed up, she was asking what had happened but no one claim to know any details, she said to grandma well if you don't mind I'll take the girls home with me tonight until we can get everything situated, Grandma said ain't nothing to be situated, these are my daughters kids and they are going with me, Ebony yelled we don't wanna go with you, we wanna go with big mama, grandma said well go with her then, but I'll be there tomorrow to get them, Ebony started packing a bag and told me to get my doll, I hardly went anywhere without her, then grandma said hold on y'all ain't taking Trina, she don't belong to y'all, she ain't your sons baby, big mama said I know that but I can take all the girls tonight, grandma said naw you ain't taking her, Ebony flew into a rage, I'm not leaving her with you, grandma jumped up and slapped her in the face yelling you are too damn grown, just then big mama said don't put your hands on that child again, the two grandma's were arguing back and forth, I was scared so I started crying, Ebony picked me up and started talking to me, she said don't cry, I may have to leave you tonight but I'm gonna call your daddy so he can come get you, I didn't want to go with grandma either I was afraid of her from previous incidents but I had no choice. Big Mama says come on girl let's go, Trina, I will call your daddy or your grandma so one of them can come to get you, I say ok as I'm standing there feeling lost and confused. I don't know what happened but daddy never came to get me, and my sisters ended up there at grandma's house with me for only a short time.

The day before mama's funeral my father stopped by to see me, had brought clothes for me to wear to the funeral, he had wanted me to color coordinate with him, so he brought me the cutest little Brown dress with Ivory trim and ivory buttons, a pair of brown knee length boots and ivory tights'. Daddy says to my grandmother who by the way is the sweetest woman in the world when he was around, but the minute he leaves I often thought that she was the devil himself he says I brought clothes for Trina to wear to the funeral and I would like her to ride with me, what time can I pick her up? Grandma says any time after 9:30 am as she is examining the clothes that daddy had brought me. So he spends a little time with me and before leaves promise to pick me up in the morning.

Grandma was what you would call nice nasty, she could be nice when she needed to be, but overall, she was just nasty, she had a quick hand that always caught you off guard, I was so afraid of her that I often prayed to God, asking him to just let me die because death had to be better than being there with her. She liked to beat me before school, I often thought that she wanted to have me scared all day, this would be her way of making sure that I was never happy or just her way of having control over me even when I wasn't in her presence. She was big on playing mind games, and when I got home she would find a reason to start up again, then she could take her time and do exactly what she wanted to do. There is no real reason for a child to get hit every single day, grandma was just a bully.

CHAPTER 8

Saying Goodbye

It's early Saturday morning, I feel weird sadder than usual but I don't know why, I just don't wanna feel anything, I don't care if I get hit, or cursed out, I don't care about anything today. It was just days of staying with grandma after mama died, that my sisters leave to go live with their dad, you see our Mother was married to their dad, she and he had split up and Mama started dating my Dad, she had never gotten a divorce from their dad, I guess that's what people did back then, and because he was Mama's husband and had signed off on his girl's birth certificates, he was free to take them away which he did. I had to stay because I was not his child. Now my dad, who did not sign my birth certificate, and I didn't have his name, will have to go thru the courts to prove paternity. He was only 31 years old and really had no experience in raising children, but he knew what he had to do.

We were all sitting on the back porch, Ebony was very emotional she was like our mom, she did everything that she could do to protect us after mama died, that's a lot of pressure for a young girl, none of us were happy and we would always lean on her because she was the next best thing to mama, it hurt her the most to have to leave me, Monica and Sheila were sad about it too and I understood even then that there was really nothing that they could do, it was just a bad situation all the way around.

Ebony said let's hold hands, as her eyes began to fill up with tears she said missy we love you and if had our way you would be going with us, Daddy says that he will bring us to visit and you can come to visit us too, Monee who was crying at this time said come here missy I went to sit in her lap, the tears are now falling from my eyes now, I look up and poor Sheila's eyes are puffy and red, her little nose is running, but she sits quietly, as usual, for a moment we all just sat there hugging and crying, Monee says as soon as I get old enough I'm gonna come back to get you, and no matter they do or say to you, you be, strong and don't let them win, ok? I shake my head yes, and I hugged her I lay my head on her shoulder, Ebony starts rubbing my head she says you know that it's going to be harder here without us, but you can't let them break you, everything that they say is a lie, you a not anything that they say you are, I'm so sorry missy I really wish that there was something that I could do, but I'm just a kid myself, I said I know that, and I will be ok, Shelia said missy you have no idea what's about to happen here, and I don't know how to explain it to you but it won't be for too long just always remember that we love you and if we could take you with us we would so when they are mean to you just find you a hiding place and take queenie with you, Ebony says Sheila don't say that you're going to scare her, I say ok Sheila, but Ebony I've been scared since we got here and the weird feeling grows, we sit there for what seems like an hour before grandma calls for Ebony, she says y'all's daddy is here come on in here and get yall's stuff together, at that time I lose the big girl facade and scream to the top of my lungs Nooooooo!!!!!! And I break and run into the house and grab a hold of his legs and I say please, please can I go, Ebony, Monee, and Sheila are right behind me all screaming and crying pleading with their dad, who says girls, girls wait for a second, he is trying to hug all of us as we crowd around him, grandma is saying something in the back ground but I'm not trying to hear anything that she is saying their dad is saying ok, girls wait for a second, stop crying, Ebony says daddy please can she go with us, we don't want to leave her here, he looks as if he wants to cry he says I would take her if I could but her father wouldn't have it, Ebb, we already talked about this he says I'm sorry missy but your dad is gonna take care of his business and he will be here to get you, we all heard him but none of us moved away from him, he picks me up and he says I will come to get you to visit sometimes ok, I'm still screaming no, no, no, the more he tries to comfort us the more we cry.

Grandma is just standing there watching she says ok now, Trina get down he has to go she tries to take me out of his arms, I grab on tighter as she is pulling me I'm grabbing onto his clothes and when she finally gets me down I run over and grab a hold to Monee, she is still crying and hugging me so tight, Ebony and Sheila ran over to where we were and the four of us just stood there hugging and crying, their dad says Ms. Millie where are their things she took him to the room where the girls had been staying, he gathered their bags and took them out to his car, grandma began to yell at us to stop it, he said please let them hug for a little while longer, she just stood there watching with this look of disgust on her face. Once he got everything in the car, he walked over to us and gently said girls it's time to go, I promise that I will bring y'all back to visit her, the girls kept hugging me I stopped crying and said ok, it's ok, you all go I will see you all later, I realized that I had to be a big girl, more for them, than myself, they each kissed me as we untangled, as they walked away I stood watching them feeling like I had died a thousand times but my heart just wouldn't stop beating, I didn't have the courage to go outside and see them get into the car, at that moment I felt like my legs wouldn't work even if I had wanted them too, grandma walked them out I heard the two of them talking, her and their dad, I heard the car doors close, I heard the car start, I heard them pull off, I just stood there staring into space, grandma said I ought to beat your ass carrying on like that, go sit down somewhere, I went into the closet and cried until I had no more tears.

Later that night before I went to bed, the phone rang and I heard grandma talking to someone, she says Trina come get this phone as I approached her she says don't be long you've got to get up early tomorrow, I said yes ma'am, I say Hello its Ebony, my heart smiles, I say hi, she says we just wanted to say goodnight, I'm shaking my head as if I was saying yes, grandma is standing behind me, she says say yea, they can't see you crazy girl, I say ok, Ebony says what did she say I answer Ebony and say nothing, Ebony's says goodnight, I love you, and I say I love you too, Monee is on the line also she says, I love you missy goodnight, I say goodnight I love you too, Sheila gets on the phone and she says missy just say yes or no, I say ok, she says did grandma say something to you when we left, I say yes, Shelia says did she hit you I said no, she says ok good, I love you missy, I say I love you, she says goodnight, I say goodnight, they all say bye, I say bye and I hang up the phone, they called me to say goodnight it was bittersweet, they called every day for a few weeks, then the calls came less and less I understood that life happened and I knew that they loved me still. But in the long run, we became estranged.

CHAPTER 9

The Beatings

5:25 am, Trina get up, I'd hear her but would be too afraid to move, I'd hear her footsteps walking towards the bed, she made me sleep with her, can you imagine being scared all night? Trina she would yell, I said get up, I'd just lay there, a few seconds later she would snatch me up from the bed and slam me to the floor, she would put her big dirty foot on my chest screaming and spitting, she had this high pitched voice that reminded me of a wicked witch, I couldn't understand what she was saying, she would be in such a rage, I couldn't make out what she was saying it was just too much going on, she is pressing that big dirty foot into my chest and stomach stomping me, her night dress is swinging wildly in the chaos and I can't help but to see her nasty nakedness as she's stomping me, yelling, and looking like a evil old lady, I can't breathe, can't escape, can't fight, feels like my nostrils are burning I'm trying to catch some air, she snatched me up from the floor, give me a few blows to head, and throw me back down to the floor, this time applying pressure to my neck choking me, squeezing harder and harder, I'm hoping that today will be the day, but of course she stops just in the nick of time I'm grasping for air, I'm crawling trying to find someplace to hide, everything is still fuzzy, my ears are ringing, I'm seeing stars, and here she comes again, she snatches me up from the floor slams me against the wall, chokes me again until I almost lose consciousness then slams my head on the wall a few times to wake me up I guess, so that I can hear her say I will kill yo ugly black ass, I will put you six feet under with your mammy, she is screaming and her face is scrolled up like something evil, I don't know what to do, I just cry but I'm thinking what did I do? Then back to the floor, I ball up in the fetal position trying to cover my head, she is kicking me, still screaming at me, then without warning, she just stops and walks away, the beating stop as suddenly as it starts, I'm able to crawl away into the closet.

I sit in the dark, crying, breathing hard scared and confused, she doesn't bother me anymore that morning, I can think of 100 ways I could kill her, while I'm sitting in the dark, if only I weren't so afraid of her, I really hated her. When I hear all of the other children up and getting ready for school I come out of the closet and try to blend in. she has clothes picked out on the bed for me to wear, I don't say anything I just get dressed, and she calls for us to eat breakfast, rice again. We were so poor and there were so many people in that house that grandma often cooked foods that she could stretch, like rice and beans. I pray that I can make it thru breakfast without incident. I sit down I'm eating when out of nowhere I'm slapped to the floor she is screaming quit sucking that food, you eat like a damn dog, I just sit there, all of the other kids are laughing and I just sit there. I hated all of them too because I didn't understand how any of that could be funny, I just sit there feeling sorry for myself, I got up and left the kitchen went to the dining room and sat under the table, grandma had a long tablecloth that drug the floor it was another hiding spot when I would hear the Flintstones intro song began to play on the TV, I knew that it was time to head out for school and When I finally get out of the house the fresh air feels like freedom, the walk to school gives me peace, at least I'll be safe for the next 8 hours. During school I didn't say much and usually kept to myself, I'd sit at my desk and do what I had to do, for the first hour or so I couldn't concentrate, my mind would be racing with what had just happened, and I'd try to block it so that I could catch on to what they were trying to teach me finally I'd get it together and everything was ok, but as 2:00 pm approached panic would set in, the last 30 minutes of school was all for nothing, I couldn't retain anything, all I could think about was what was going to happen when I got back to that house, I'd be so nervous I could literally feel myself shaking. I remember the day when the teacher said Katrina are you ok? I stood there staring at her while I was trying to decide what I wanted to say, did I want to tell her everything and take a chance that it would backfire on me and they would just tell grandma what I've said, or would they do something about it? because lawd knows I remember the last beating I got for telling somebody what goes on in her house, Hmmm, let me see I had no faith in grown-ups, they couldn't be trusted so I decided to say yes I'm ok, I figured I had a better chance of just letting things be.

On a good day and if the weather was nice she would be sitting on the porch which meant that I might be ok, she could possibly be in a good mood, but if she was in the house watching her stories as she called it, I could be in grave danger. It was very hard to predict what would really happen because she was very unpredictable, I never really got it down to a science, so in the best case, I always retreated to the closet. On the walk, home I'm praying God please let me escape a beating today, and I say thank you to Jesus about 100 times afterward, I thought that if I said thank you to Jesus many times that he would definitely hear my prayers, sometimes he heard me most times he didn't so I thought.

CHAPTER 10

Queenie

That same weekend, I was on the back porch playing with my dog queenie, she was the only one that I felt I had a connection with, while were playing she is licking my face and I'm laughing and trying to push her away, grandma was in the kitchen, I guess the sound of my laughter disturbed her because she swung open the kitchen door, screaming my name "Trina get your nasty ass up from there letting that dog lick you all in the mouth" he wasn't licking me in the mouth he was licking my face, that was her the big liar, she always made things seem far worse than they were, she startled me and queenie both we just sat there, she lounged towards me and grabbed my arm and before she could pick me up from the porch Queenie jumped up on her leg as if she was pushing her away from me, she barked, growled and showed her teeth, I guess that she too was tired of grandma beating me, she usually would bark or growl, but she had never jumped up on grandma's leg before, when it would start she would pace the floor barking but never really intervened like she did this day, even then she never tried to bite grandma, she just wanted her to stop bothering me, Queenie stood in between us and continued growling until grandma backed off, grandma said as she walked away "ooh ok, I see, you wanna bite me, I've got something for you, you damn mutt" and laughs this evil laugh and goes into the house, I tell queenie that were in trouble now, we go into the house and into the closet, a few moments later the closet door opens and my grandma goons are grabbing queenie out of the closet she is trying to fight them off but she just can't, I'm crying leave her alone, my grandma grabs my leg and pulls me out of the closet she says so you told your dog to bite me, I screaming no I didn't, as she slaps me a few times, she has one hand around the back of my neck the other repeatedly hitting me about the head and face, she drags me back to the back porch, where I see the goons tying a rope around queenie's neck, poor doggy, she is trying to get away, she can't, I'm scared it's so much noise, Queenie is crying, barking, growling, the goons are laughing and scuffling with her, grandma is hitting me and cursing I wish that I would just disappear, finally they get the rope around her neck and they hang her, grandma is making me watch telling me that's what they are going to do to me, she makes me watch until queenie stops kicking her legs, she is dead, they drop her body to the hard ground, I can still hear the thump, she lets me go, I run into the closet, I'm crying I say Jesus, they killed queenie she was a good girl, she was my only friend, why Jesus did you let them kill her? Jesus didn't answer me, I lay down on the floor I'm crying and the tears are filling up my ears it was uncomfortable but I deserve to be uncomfortable, because of me, my queenie had to die. Why did I run to the closet? I should have just taken her and ran down the alley, or maybe gone into the basement, I should have done anything but take her to the closet, it's all my fault.

I stay in the closet for the rest of the night, she doesn't send for me and I don't come out, sometime during the night I asked Jesus again if I could just please go to be with him, queenie was there, mama was there, I would be safe again. Jesus never answered me that night, I thought maybe he was mad at me too. I just wanted to die, just like Mama, Just like Queenie. They were the lucky ones.

CHAPTER 11

The Funeral

The morning of the funeral, my grandma who was nice this morning called me into the bathroom, she says were gonna let your cousin wear the clothes that your daddy brought for you because she doesn't have anything to wear, it's such a pretty dress she would look better in it anyway, I just stood there thinking to myself is she asking me this? She then says you're going to wear this, it's a skirt that grandma made for you. It was a curtain that she sewed into a skirt she put an ivory turtle neck with it, I didn't say a word I put on this ensemble which by the way was a homemade hot mess, to say the least. But honestly, I didn't care I was just excited about seeing daddy and riding in the car with him, just being with him made me feel like I was someone, it felt like being full of love like he would open me up and pour in love till it overflowed and going back be with grandma was like being opened up and turned upside down letting it all flow out, she kept me on empty. I remembered the conversation that she had with daddy, she told him that he could come by 9:30 and it was barely 8:15 and we were leaving, so I said grandma, my daddy is coming for me and I want to wait for him, Grandma say well he ain't here he's late, we don't have time to wait for him, I said you told him 9:30?, I knew that saying anything to her was gonna buy me a beating later on, but I didn't care because the reality was I was gonna get one anyway I just wanted to be with my daddy. Grandma says oh you have a voice now, you wait till later smart mouth you just wait, and what you know about the time, she chuckles I've got something for you. I just looked at her for some reason at that moment I didn't fear her. I just stood there and looked at her.

We pull up to the funeral home, go inside and sit down, I'm looking for my daddy, the funeral starts when I hear daddy's voice I jump up and go sit with him, he says what are you wearing? Why don't you have on the clothes that I brought you? I tell him what grandma says he just sat there.

After the funeral, everyone was paying their respect to the family, daddy and I walk over to grandma and he says Ms. Millie why isn't Trina wearing the clothes that I brought for her, grandma snapped and says this ain't the time or the place for you to be asking me about no damn clothes, she ain't wearing it because I didn't want her to wear it as she pushed past daddy, he was mad but being the man that he was he took me by the hand and we left the funeral home. On the car ride to the repast, I began to tell him all about the beatings and everything that has happened, He just listens as I talk, he says daddy will take care of it, I'm happy I'm hoping that he will just take me away from her house today, then he started to explain that because he and my mom weren't married and that his name was not on my birth certificate that he had to prove who he was to the courts and that it would be just a little longer.

The repast was at grandma's house after everyone had left I watched grandma as she was cleaning, I was silently praying that she would stay as nice as she had pretended to be while everyone was there, praying that the sorrow from losing her daughter would somehow change her. My dad says can I speak to you for a moment, talking to grandma, Grandma says I don't want to talk about no damn clothes, No its more serious than that, he says, Missy told me about what's been going on over here all the beatings and the mistreatment, he says I hope that she is exaggerating because I can't make myself understand how you could do a child like that, she response I discipline her when needed and will continue to do so, but there is nothing excessive, you know how kids are they like to play grown-ups against each other, that's my dead daughters baby, then she paused as if she had to push back her tears all that I have left of my child, the older girls wanted to be with their daddy, and I couldn't stop it because if I had my way I would have kept the girls together, daddy says I understand that, but please keep in mind that she is just a baby and she has just lost her mother please cut her some slack, Grandma says umm-hmm, daddy kisses me goodbye he says I'll be here Friday to get you, I began to cry daddy please don't leave me, daddy says don't do me like this, don't cry baby daddy wouldn't leave you if he didn't have too, he picks me up and he says in my ear, it's gonna be alright.

She ain't gonna bother you no more daddy talked to her, I knew that he had no clue as to what was going to happen to me, at that moment I wished that I had just kept my mouth shut because I knew that I was gonna get it, so I hugged my daddy's neck tight and took in a deep breath, mentally preparing myself for the wrath of grandma. He put me down both grandma and I walked him out they were making small talk and grandma was squeezing my hand so tight I knew that I was in trouble, Daddy got into the car and pulled off as soon as he turned the corner before we could walk back into the house, slap right in the face, there was that quick right that always seems to catch me in the eye, I immediately cover my head and brace myself for the next blow, she shoves me towards the front door my sixty pound body crashes into the door, I'm pushing the door trying to get in the house before she can hit me again, too late feels like a fist in the small of my back, I manage to get up run into the house, I'm not fast enough grandma is screaming catch her, Goon number one intercepts, holding me and laughing, grandma says get me a belt, goon number two takes his off she puts my head in between her legs and she starts to beat me with the belt, I'm trapped in funky hot space, I can't breath and I can't shield myself from the blows to my backside, she throws me down to the floor and she grabs my lips and she pulls them, twisting them and says what goes on in my damn house stays in my God Damn house do you understand me? before striking the last blow, a closed hand punch to my nose, which started bleeding almost instantly, she then starts yelling you better not bleed on my floor, I'm dizzy my vision is blurry, I don't know what to do, I'm crawling to the bathroom she picks up from the floor yelling hold your head back, she grabs my little ponytails pulling my head back, she does it so hard it feels like she snapped my neck, she takes a wet rag and slaps it on my face rubbing my nose so hard I just want to pass out.

When she finally stops the bleeding, she is calm now she says take off those clothes so that I can wash them, I'm feeling woozy but I do what I'm told she gives me some clothes to put on, I just wanna lay down she says you can't go to sleep so she makes me do jumping jacks, my little body is about to give out when I say underneath my breath Jesus, can I come now please and suddenly I felt like I had been recharged my strength had returned, I really didn't understand why that was at that time, but I know now that there is power in the name of Jesus. When she finally let me lay down before falling asleep I vowed to never tell daddy anything else.

CHAPTER 12

The Stabbing

Mama, Mary, and Charlene were in the car headed to the bar, Charlene says to Mary I left my wallet at your place we need to stop by and get it, and they stopped by Mary's apartment. Mary lived in a housing project, they were newly built it was fairly nice, it was across the street from Mount Sinai Hospital, that hospital I know because whenever Mama would take to us Mary's place she would say missy that's the hospital where you were born, and I'd ask her to tell me the story of my birth, time and time again, each time I asked she would tell me. At the building where Mary lived there were always guys standing around outside of the building sometimes they were gambling or just hanging out. As the ladies walked past Mary who knew most of the guys by name was speaking and Charlene said come on girl, why are you out here talking to these hoodlums, I'm not trying to get robbed, Charlene was always thinking that she was better than most and felt that everyone would always want something from her. No one knew exactly how she got her money or the things that she possessed because she didn't work, however, there were many rumors, one of her being a prostitute, the other a drug runner but no one knew exactly.

Mama chimed in and said she had better get to know them they will protect her if she ever needed them. Charlene said Ora please girl you don't know what you're talking about they will be the first to do something to her; Mama said I could be wrong but I don't believe that. Once they were in the apartment Charlene went into the kitchen and got a beer from the fridge, Mary said girl you better stay out of my shit, besides, we were just coming to get your wallet, and were leaving, Charlene said girl your so damn petty it's just a beer, Mary said MY beer, hell when you do let us come to your place we can't even get past the living room without you having something to say but you're always in our house like you own it, especially mine. Charlene says yes, I do because everything you got up in here my man brought, you thought that I didn't know huh? Mary just looked at her and said girl there you go again with that, I already told you that wasn't true. Mama said I thought that you all had gotten over that, come on let's go please because I'm not in the mood for no more drama tonight. Charlene said it ain't going to be no drama, I'm just telling this Ho that I know about her fucking my man, Mary said whatever Charlene and tried to walk past her to leave the kitchen, Charlene pushed Mary and Mary pushed her back, Mama jumped in between her two sisters and said come on now let's just go, were sisters, and we don't let no man come in between us at all, Charlene why are you looking like that? oh lord, girl please do not start any mess, let that go, it's not worth it! at that time Charlene snapped and told Mama girl shut the fuck up with your wanna be righteous ass, old peace-making ass Super savior or somebody, Mary said this bitch is crazy she goes from hot to cold in a split second, Mama said this makes no sense, Charlene said no seriously Mary are you fucking Charles, Mary just chuckled and said I'm not gonna do this with you again, as she lit a cigarette, Charlene said somebody just told me that he just brought you a washing machine and dryer, Mary said well somebody just lied to you,Charlene yelled I know that you're lying you've always wanted what I have, I'm gonna find out for sure, and if he did buy it I'm gonna fuck you up, you yellow bitch!! Mary says that's the problem Charlene, you mad because you see how your man watches me, you need to be talking to him instead of always throwing threats ain't nobody scared of you and ain't nobody messing with your man, you need to get on with that! Let me ask you something, are you jealous of me Charlene? at that time Charlene reached around Mama and punched Mary in the face, Mary of course started swinging and Mama who was in the middle started to push Charlene back to break up the fight, Charlene then grabbed a blade from her bra and swung the blade and slashed Mama across the neck, hitting her carotid artery as blood sprayed her in the face, Mama grabbed her neck and slid down the refrigerator down to the floor, Mary was afraid she stood flush against the kitchen wall and watched, Charlene then spit in Mama's face and said die bitch with your peacemaking ass, turned towards Mary and said you're gonna be next let me find out about you and Charles as she turned and ran towards the door of the apartment, she grabbed the keys and padlock from the table, she slammed the door shut and put the lock on the burglar bars and ran down the stairs.

Mary grabbed the phone to call the police she then got a towel to try to stop the blood from spraying, Mama was losing a lot of blood, Hello I need an ambulance my sister just got stabbed, the operator begins to ask her a series of questions Mary who is in full panic mode says please just come now she was stabbed in the neck, and there is so much blood, she looks like she is gonna pass out, please hurry and she hangs up the phone. Mary thought that she could get the guys to just carry Mama across the street instead of waiting for the ambulance so she went to the door to run down to get them but the bars were locked she ran frantically around the living room looking for the keys to unlock the bars, all the while crying and saying hold on sister I'm gonna get you some help, she went to the window and started calling them to help, one of the guys heard her, he yelled back what's going on red, Mary says my sister has been stabbed we need to get across the streets to the hospital, the guys they break and run up the stairs to the apartment door, Mama is still sitting on the floor in the kitchen a small pool of blood is forming around her, she can barely breathe she is clawing at the wall she is trying to get up. The guys get to the door but can't get the bars open they are beating the lock with a mallet, there is a lot of commotion, and they are doing all that they could do to break the padlock from the burglar bars, at this time the police and the fire department shows up, they had the tools to cut the lock and get into the apartment., By the time they got mama across the streets to the hospital, she was pronounced dead on arrival, she had lost t00 much blood.

Charlene ran down the three flights of stairs out of the building past the guys, who had just seen her go into the building, one of them noticed what appeared to be blood on her face, it was dark so he couldn't be sure, he said to her ma'am are you ok? Charlene who did not respond kept running, so they didn't give it much thought and kept on with what they were doing, Charlene ran into the park which was behind the building she paced back and forth, her mind was racing, she didn't have a plan she didn't know what to do. She was so caught up in trying to figure out what just happened that she didn't even notice the two men who had walked up on her they saw all the blood on her face, neck, and blouse they said are you ok, and she didn't respond, at that time she heard the police siren which broke her from her trance and she started to run away the two men ran behind her caught her and asked her what was going on, and all that she said was let me go, I didn't mean to stab her, stab who one of the guys said, Charlene said Ora, one of the two men told the other go see what was going on, I'm staying with her. As the guy approached the building there were police officers who were questioning people, he told them about the woman in the park, the paramedics and a few uniformed officers took off running towards the park, where they saw Charlene running away, they gave chase and a few moments later they were walking back with Charlene who was in handcuffs. It seems as if all of the remorse that she displayed to the two strangers in the park had vanished because she was trash-talking to the police Charlene was taken to the police station for questioning, she flat out refused to talk about what had happened between her and her sister, they sat there for hours trying to get a confession but no luck, she would not say a word regarding the incident but had no problem with cursing them out, she sat there with the dried blood on her skin and clothes, it wasn't until they told her that they were going to take pictures and that she needed to change her clothes that she broke out into a panic and begin crying uncontrollably. They had also taken Mary down to the station for questioning, The detective says Mary, I'm sorry for the loss of your sister, and I know that this a sensitive time for you, but I need to ask you these questions while it's still fresh on your mind, Mary says ok, she starts by saying I always knew that Charlene was going to hurt one of us one day, the detective says why Mary do you say that, Mary says because she is always fighting with us, not just me and my sister but with my brothers too, she's evil, earlier tonight we went to my sister's house to get our hair done, Charlene jumped on my sister then because she didn't like the way my sister raises her kids, Mary just sat there and stared crying, she says thru her tears, my sister has four kids, who is gonna take care of her kids, the detective says I know this hurts but it will be ok, Mary says my sister is dead because of me, the detective say what do you mean Mary, Mary says we were arguing Charlene and I, Ora got in between us to break up the fight, when Charlene hit me, Ora started pushing her back to stop us from fighting, then Charlene pulled the blade out and cut my sister, Mary got up from the table started walking around the interrogation room she broke down and started crying. In another part of the building while waiting in a holding cell Charlene had a mental break and was placed in a physiatrist hospital; until she would be able to stand trial for the murder.

CHAPTER 13

The Insurance Policy

Today is the day that grandma is expecting to receive the check for the life insurance policy for the death of mama, I didn't know how much it was worth, nor was that any of my business that was a grownup thing, I would hear them talking about what they were going to do with the money when it came, I really didn't understand I just knew that grandma was the beneficiary and that she was expecting it that day, she got up early, she is in a good mood, I'm happy that she is happy, maybe today will be a good day, she cleans the house and prepares breakfast, no rice, it was grits, no beating this morning, made it thru breakfast, guess that I wasn't eating like a dog today. I got to pick my own clothes; there was actually no tension in the house, she usually had an attitude in the mornings she was just mad all the time, always yelling, hitting, and cursing mainly towards me but today was different, it was good, I walked to school feeling free. I had the best day ever, but again as 2:00 pm approached panic sets in, I couldn't stop it, I knew in my heart that today was too good to be true, that I'm gonna get it double when I get home. the walk home from school was bittersweet, I was more nervous than usual because I really didn't know what to expect, but to my surprise when I made it to the house no one was there and that was not a usual thing, it was always a full house, I was just gonna take advantage of the moment, I made myself some peanut butter and jelly crackers and turned on the TV, I was able to watch the

Flintstones in peace and eat without hesitation, it really was a good day. I paid no mind to the other children or to what they were doing, it was every man for himself and I was loving it.

It was shortly after our arrival from school that they all arrived back at the house, it's funny how money can put you in a good mood, everyone is happy they all had been shopping, Grandma was in a good mood, her voice was different when she asked me what I had learned in school that day, she often asked me that question, and it usually leads to a slap or a series of degrading words, but not today, She asked and I answered and she left me alone, hmmm I thought what is this all about, I didn't like getting hit or cursed out but when it didn't happen I felt more afraid because this meant that she was changing her routine and that scared me, now I'm kind of disappointed because I was sure that when I got home that I would get it worst because she had missed this morning, trying not to work myself up in a frenzy, wishing that she would just do it already because the stress of waiting on it was just as worst as the licks themselves, so I just took a seat and waited.

Mary was pulling out everything that she had gotten for them, for her and her kids, and my Grandma and her two goons were pulling out their new clothes and shoes, I just sat and waited to see what I had if anything, as I sat there waiting patiently grandma said, so nonchalantly Trina I'll get you something tomorrow, I couldn't remember your size. Disappointed but not surprised, I acted if it didn't bother me and continued to watch what everyone else had, Later that night she would order pizza and soda, that was a rare treat, I was really excited about it so as I waited to get a slice, and suddenly here we go, grandma yelled Trina why are you acting like you've never had pizza before, I answered with I'm sorry, I don't know what I did, but she got up walked over to where I was and snatched me out of the line of kids waiting to get pizza, slung me across the kitchen, as I was sliding on the floor she yelled at me you're not getting none but you're gonna sit here and watch everyone else eat, I sat on the floor with tears in my eyes, I was so hungry and the pizza smelled so good, after everyone was done grandma said get up from there and clean up this mess, I stated scraping the plates into the trash, I pulled a chair to the sink to wash the dishes, I would slide my finger along the plates to get the sauce and lick my fingers hoping that she wouldn't see me, and after the dishes were done I took the garbage bag out to the back yard while walking down the stairs I pulled out a few pieces of the crust that someone had left on their plate, I put one in my mouth and three more in my pocket, I walked back into the house and into the closet where I could eat the other pieces of crust. That night was the first night that she had not let me eat but it would be the beginning of an almost daily thing. I realized that she would do it mostly over the weekend; she was determined to starve me. Because I could always eat at school, and if some of the other children didn't want their food I could eat theirs too.

The next day they all got up and going again, it was welfare check and food stamp day, they would walk to the currency exchange stand in line to get their welfare checks cashed and pick up the envelope of food stamps, then they would go to the grocery store, where they would buy can goods by the cases, and it was always the same thing, sweet kernel corn, sweet cream corn, green beans, Lima beans, mixed vegetables, pork N beans, and Vienna sausage, and tomato paste, the pantry looked like the shelves in the stores the freezer and the refrigerator would be jammed packed, it always seemed like so much food but it never lasted for more than a few weeks, the last week before it was food stamp day again we would have nothing, pantry bout bare, nothing in the fridge but mayonnaise, and pickle relish.

Once all of the groceries were put away, we kids were outside playing in front of the house, and the grownups were sitting on the porch, drinking beer and smoking cigarettes, grandma didn't drink or smoke but she liked to dip snuff, which I thought was disgusting, but it suited her because I thought that she was just as disgusting. When this box truck pulls up, the driver gets out of the truck, goes up to the door, and grandma signs a form, a few moments later the driver and his helper pulled out a brand new pool table. Which they took down to the basement, it was a gift for the goons, it was Christmas in July, they were really excited and were sure to tell us, kids, not to touch it.

CHAPTER 14

Garbage Picker

It wasn't long before all of the money ran out and things had gotten back to normal, I was getting beaten and starved on a regular basis by now, and eating out of the trash can became my thing to do, I'm standing there trying to figure out how I'm going to do this, for dinner tonight she cooked spaghetti and neck bones all in the same pot, nothing really to take from the trash, it was just neck bones, spaghetti noodles and tomato sauce so I'm gonna have to somehow try to lick the plates before they go in the sink, I'm usually more cleaver but today somehow I slipped and one of my cousins saw me, she says ewe that's nasty I'm telling, I try to plead with her please don't tell, she takes off yelling grandma Trina is licking the plates, I'm scared to death, I hear her coming down the hallway, she is yelling are you licking the plates? I lie, no I'm just washing the dishes she snatches me out of the chair and says open your mouth, she smells my breath, and operation beat down is in full effect, I hated her, I hated my cousins more, I hated the goons and everyone else that stood by and allowed her to mistreat me. I took that beating like I had so many times before and retreated to the closet. As I sit there in the dark, I pray dear God, I'm ready to die now, and can you please take me to be with you? I fall asleep in the closet she doesn't send for me, I wake up in the night, the house is still, it's quiet, I've never seen it like this before I'm walking thru the house everyone is sleep, everywhere on the floor, the couches, everywhere, I feel so powerful I walk past grandma's bedroom, I look at her asleep, even then she looks evil, I keep walking towards the kitchen, I want to open the refrigerator but I'm thinking the light might give me away, I realize that I can trust no one, so I go into the pantry there has to be something that I can eat, I'm too short I can't reach the first shelf, there is a phone book on the floor I stand on it, I can reach something, a can of something, I grab it and walk to the dish drawer hoping that the can opener is on top, so that I won't have to move around the utensils, don't want to wake anyone, I find it and I go back to the closet, its dark, can't tell what it is, I partially open the can, I smell it, its corn, its sweet creamed corn, I drink it, the entire can, I feel better, I take the can and the can opener and I hide them in a box in the closet, I pull a coat down and lay in it and go back to sleep, I WIN.

Corn, Corn, Corn, corn, and I became close friends; grandma would always say what is going on with this corn, it seems to be disappearing, I would laugh on the inside feeling like I had something over her.

CHAPTER 15

The Almost Drowning

I'm outside playing with my cousins, grandma is standing on the porch, and she calls my name, I hated the way that she said my name, I say ma'am? She says come here and help me get these clothes hung up, I take the long walk up the stairs into the house, I walk thru the house to the back porch she has a basket of jeans that needs to be hung out on the line we have a washing machine but no dryer, we usually wash the clothes and then hang them on the clothes line in the back yard, she says, grab that stick and set up the line, the stick is a long two by four piece of wood board we use it to hold the clothes line high enough so that the clothes don't drag the ground, I take the stick and I push it up high, I realize that it may be too high for me but I'm trying to make it tall enough for her, while standing there trying to gauge the height, out of nowhere she slaps me across the face, "you know that's too damn high, slap me again, I don't have time for your stupid ass today, you better fix it and fix it quick before I beat your black ass" my ears are ringing I'm seeing stars I quickly kick the stick so that it will fall so that I can adjust it, while the tears are streaming down my face, I want to scream but I'm paralyzed in fear, I stand there with my head down bracing myself for the next blow, and in my mind I've hit her with this stick a thousand times, if only I could defend myself a few second later she says go get the clothes pins from the porch, I run to the porch as soon as I reach the stairs I rub my face and ears somehow trying to make it feel better but I don't want her to see me, I get the clothes pins I say grandma here are the clothes pins, she yells' well start hanging the damn clothes, and you better not drop them, I'm nervous the anxiety is too much, Imagine being a skinny 6 year old, that weighs about 60 lbs.trying to hang a wet pair of jeans that belongs to a grown man, I silently say Jesus can you help me? He did because I didn't drop not one pair, there's that power again, power in the name of Jesus. We go down into the basement to start another load, she says go turn the hot water tank to high, high as it can get the water isn't hot enough, I said ok as I walk over to the tank, I turn it to high, we continue to wash and hang clothes after it was done I was allowed to go back to play. Later that night when it was time for dinner I was waiting to see if I would be able to eat, or if I would have to steal my corn once everyone was asleep. It was a good day I was able to eat and sit at the table to eat without incident, and that scarred me, I feel like something bigger is brewing in her mind because she is being nice.

Its 5am, grandma snatches me out of the bed, and she's on her usual rampage, again she's screaming about something that I've done, which is just an excuse to beat me, in her mind I deserve this beating, she dragging me by my little hair with one hand, she has my shirt in the other hand dragging me towards the bathroom, I'm scared, my heart is beating fast, not knowing what is going to happen this time, no matter how many times I get beat I'm never quite ready for it, I'm crying and yelling I'm saying sorry grandma please don't whoop me, please I'm sorry, we get to the bathroom she slings up against the tub, I'm lying on the floor scared, looking around trying to figure out what she's doing she is talking in her normal voice, she is saying I got something for your black ass now, she is putting on those yellow rubber cleaning gloves, I'm so scared I don't know what to do, don't know what she is going to do, she grabs another pair starts to put them on one on top of the other, the door is open, I try to crawl out of the bathroom past her, she catches me and started choking me, I'm thinking yes do it, kill me, but she stops and she is looking down at me, this is a look that I've never seen before her face is relaxed now she actually looks peaceful which scares me more, all of this is new, I don't know what to think, she grabs me by my hair and she lifts me up from the floor, I can feel the hair pulling from the scalp, I'm face to face with the bathtub, its full of water, its hot water, I can see the smoke coming from it, I understand what's happening now why she put the gloves on, I try to get away but I couldn't she slams my head into the bathtub, then dunks my head first in the hot water its hot, its burning, I can't breathe, now she is yelling, I'm fighting to get my head out of the tub, pushing back against the tub trying to pull my head out, she is too strong her grip is too strong, I can't, she pulls me out screams something in my face and down into water I go again, only this time I don't fight I wanna die, I hear my uncle say Mama what are you doing? We she lets me go he pulls me up, he pushes her up against the wall he says it stops now! don't put your hands on this girl again, he says come on bird face, that's what he used to call me, I can't go with him, I can't move, my face is burned there is blood I'm sitting on the floor trying to catch my breath, he stands there they both are looking at me, he says to her, look what you did to her, how are you gonna fix it? He picks me up from the floor and sits me on the toilet, he takes my T-shirt off he says let me see where you're burned, he says basically her face she is growing blisters on her face and neck he says give me some Vaseline, grandma goes to get it before she comes back the blisters has formed there is one big blister over my right eye, I mean my eye is inside of the blister, she comes back into the bathroom still wearing the gloves, she digs into the Vaseline jar and slaps me in the face with so much force that she pushes my head back, my heads slams up against that back of the toilet, she is rubbing this Vaseline in my face bursting the blisters it's burning worse I'm crying she is screaming shut up, my uncle again says Mama, just leave I'll do it, he tried as best he could not to hurt me anymore but it burned as I sat there and he applied the Vaseline. My Uncle takes me from the bathroom to the living room where he slept, he put me on one of his T-shirts he said lay down, and he walked away he says to grandma now what are you gonna do? Did you see her face? you need to get some cocoa butter or aloe Vera, your gonna keep this up and you're going to jail? Grandma didn't respond.

CHAPTER 16

Uncle

My Uncle was the nicest person that you could ever meet, he had children of his own but he took time out with all of us kids and everyone had their own nickname, and my name was bird face, he said that I looked like a little bird, whenever he was around he took special care of me, he would make sure that I ate; he was the only one who would protect me from grandma. My Uncle was sick he had been diagnosed with TB, (Tuberculosis) after that he was around a lot. He slept on the sleeper sofa in the Living room, he would cough a lot but he would still take time out for us kids, as his illness progressed he wasn't as active, he mainly laid down watching TV I felt safe with him being there, I would often spend my day sitting on his bed watching TV with him, he would say bird face go get me some water, and of course, I'd do it, he'd ask me to go to the store to get him some lemons, he would suck on the lemons, I think that they somehow soothed his cough, he had a trash can near his bed where he would spit out mucus it had a very distinctive scent it smelled like lemons and medicine to me. I loved him and I know that he loved me, I asked him once can I pray for you? He said what do you know about that? I said I don't know, he smiled and he said yes, I said ok, now fold your hands and close your eyes, I prayed Dear Jesus, make my uncle well again stop him from, coughing and if you won't do that please let him go home with you, please give him special powers to keep me safe from grandma, if you take him home with you and

Jesus please don't let him be sick when he goes to your house, thank you, Jesus, amen. I opened my eyes and my Uncle was staring at me, he said I'm sorry that Mama is so mean to you, I'm sorry that I couldn't always protect you, he said I'd heard about what was going on but I was too busy with my own life, he said will you forgive me? I said yes and then told him to say Amen. My uncle passed away shortly after that, and whenever the beating would start I swear I could smell that lemon scent and somehow the beatings weren't that bad.

C H A P T E R   17

The Truancy Officer

So I missed school for a few weeks, after the almost drowning I don't know what she told the school about me not going, but I overheard her telling my dad, that I was sick with a fever and an ear ache that I could not go with him that weekend, according to her my dad said that he was coming by to see me and I better not tell him what happened, he never came or maybe she lied and told him that I wasn't there, all I know is that it was a long time before I saw him again. I was lying where my uncle used to sleep on the sofa when there was a knock on the door, it was the truancy officer, my grandma told me to get under the dining room table and I had better not say a word, I did what I was told she opened the door, hello he said, my name is Mr. Danbury I work CPS, I'm the truancy officer for area 5, I'm here to check on Katrina Wade, according to our records she has missed 6 days of school, grandma said oh yes come on in, I sent word to the schoolhouse that Trina was real sick, you see she has these tubes in her ears and she keeps an ear infection, which causes her to have a fever The truancy officer says ok, where is she, grandma says she is asleep she had just taken her medicine, do you want me to wake her? The truancy officer said no that won't be necessary, but when do you expect that she will be back in school? grandma says oh by Monday or Tuesday, oh ok he says well here is my card call me if something should change he says, do you mind if I sit down for a minute to write my notes, grandma says sure, he sits right at

49

the table that I'm under, I want to touch his leg just to get his attention but I'm scared of what would happen, I can't make myself touch him, I just sit there scared. I'm sitting under the table and screaming on the inside help me, help me, please. But I'm too afraid to use my words. He says ok that will do it, thank you, grandma says no problem while opening the door to let him out, thank you, have a good day she says, there goes that nice nasty again. she was so sure of herself that she had struck so much fear in me that I wouldn't dare say a word. I was upset and disappointed that I couldn't or wouldn't help myself. She was right!

I stay under the table while grandma is talking to my Aunt Mary as they watch All My Children, I hate soap operas.

As my skin heals it's a little blotchy and I notice that it seems to glow not like before it's like new skin and I like, it's still sensitive to touch I can apply the aloe Vera directly from the plant, the gel is cool and it soothes my skin. Its Monday morning, I can go back to school, I'm happy to get out of the house, while I'm getting dressed my grandma comes up close to me and she says listen at me good, you go down to that school house and whoever asks you, you tell them that you were sick with the ear infection, if you tell anybody bout what happened I swear I'll kill you, that didn't scare me, actually I thought about telling just so she would do it. I said yes ma'am, I could never look her in the eyes I was always afraid that the devil would jump out of her eyes into mine, I didn't want to be the devil.

CHAPTER 18

The Letter

One Saturday I'm sitting on the porch the mailman comes, and he hands me the mail, I go into the house, and I said grandma the mail is here, I'm scared that she might hit me I brace myself, she says why are you flinching? She says just says give it here and snatches it from me almost snatching my arm out of the socket, I walk away thinking she is evil, asking me why, I'm flinching, duh because I don't wanna get hit stupid. I go back to the porch, I hear her cursing and going on about my dad how he is no good, and all he wants is the social security check and how she needed that money to pay her bills, she is mad and damning him to hell, then she opens another letter that says that Charlene will be released soon, she starts going on again, I'm sitting there like dang, I'm going to get it and good today,!!! panic sets in what can I do? where can I go? I've got nothing, I just wait on it. Grandma calls me into the house she starts telling me about how we have to go to the courthouse and they are going to test me to see if my daddy is my daddy, she says, and if those white folks ask you where you wanna live you tell them that you wanna stay with grandma you hear me? I say yes ma'am, she says you don't want to stay with David he knows nothing bout no kids plus he doesn't want you all he is after is your social security check, I hated when she talked about my daddy because in my mind he was the best thing walking the earth. She says you tell them that you are happy here and you better not tell them bout nothing that goes on in my damn house! Do you understand me? I say yes Ma'am, I'm thinking as soon as they ask I'm telling everything, I'm getting excited no more corn, no more beatings, I think I started daydreaming and smiling, but a slap to the face brought me back to reality, grandma is yelling what the hell you standing there grinning like a chest cat for? Did I say something funny, I say no, then what the hell are you grinning at? I just stand there she grabs me by my shirt right at the base of the neck, I can feel her knuckles in my throat and she said go down there and do something stupid if you want to, there will be nothing or nobody too keep me off of your ass, I swear I'll put you six feet under with your mammy, I just stand there like really how can I respond to that? Grandma is sitting there staring at me, her face is beginning to ball up I know that look, oh too well, she starts screaming UGH, I hate you as she picks me up and throws me against the wall, as I hit the floor I take flight, I run as fast as I can, out of the front door she can't catch me I win, for that moment. I run thru the alley past one of the goons he and his friends who are playing basketball he says Trina where are you going I keep running, and at that time I hear my grandma's voice catch her, she's yelling I'm praying Jesus to pick me up, make me disappear or something because I know that I can't outrun the goon, I hear him gaining on me but I don't stop, he catches me and he is laughing, he says you're gonna get it what did you do? I didn't respond I was just trying to fight to get free, I hated him too, he was one of her imps, he was holding on to me too tight, I bit him and he punched me in the face, I couldn't tell if he hit me in my nose or my mouth because they were both hurting I felt the warm blood from my nose running down my face but I tasted blood inside my mouth also, as he approached my grandma who was in the alley waiting he said she bit me Mama and I hit her I didn't mean to make her bleed, grandma snatched me out of his arms as she replied to him, you should have knocked her ass out, then a slap across the face and out of my mouth came one of my top teeth and a mouth full of blood, once inside the house she took me to the bathroom she was screaming what's wrong with you bleeding all over my damn house as she choked me screaming open your mouth and let me see, I couldn't understand why she was saying that when my mouth was open gasping for air, she stopped chocking me and started jamming my head down in the sink telling me to catch some water, but the water was flowing on the back of my head, the goon was standing in the door way looking, I didn't know what the look on his face meant, I couldn't tell if it was empathy or satisfaction. Eventually, she let me rinse my mouth and she held my head back to stop the nose bleed, both my lips were swollen, they already looked like little duck beaks, she says go sit yo ass down somewhere, and I went to my closet.

CHAPTER 19

Charlene Comes Home

The morning Charlene comes home the house is in a bittersweet mood, grandma and her other kids aren't exactly happy, they aren't sad it was just a weird vibe, I'm not knowing much about Charlene and remembering the last time that I saw her that she had gotten into a fight with my Mama and I heard them say that she was the one who had killed my mama as well, I didn't know what to feel, I just waited to see what would happen, she comes thru the door, she is happy speaking to everyone looking around, she sees me and the smile drops from her face, I just stand there, then she proceeds to speak to everyone as if I wasn't there, everyone is sitting around while she is telling stories from her time on the crazy ward, it was weird as everyone seemed different because she was there, for the first time I saw fear in grandma's face, I realized that everyone was afraid of her, on the inside I'm happy they all needed to be scared I'm thinking maybe I can join forces with her and no one would mess with me, ha-ha I'm thinking that's a grand idea, but how can I pull it off.

Not long after she had gotten home a man come to pick her up, when she left they all sat around talking about her and how they wished that she had not gotten out, I just sat and listened trying to get all the information that I could so that I could somehow devise a plan on how to get in on her good side. I understood that she had killed my Mother and that I should be mad at her, but I was trying to survive. While she was out grandma had fixed a room up for her in the basement and put all of her things in the room that she had brought back with her, she had this book wrapped in a white towel, I heard grandma and them talking about how no one could touch it, that it was scared, I just watched and listened. Charlene came back with lots of bags this man had taken her shopping and as she was talking about where she had gone and what designer outfits she had she seemed very happy about her things, everyone sat around and watched and listened like she was a celebrity, Charlene said well let me get dressed so that I could go out for a while I feel like a caged bird, I need to flap my wings everyone laughed a nervous laugh, Charlene said what is wrong with y'all, everyone says nothing, Charlene says Mary come down here and help me do my hair, Mary said we were about to go so she gathered up her kids and they left. Charlene went to the basement, when she came back up she had gotten dressed and was ready to go, I walked up to her trying to break the ice, I said you look very pretty she looked at me rolled her eyes, and walked away, I watched her walk away and thought your not pretty anyway, dang I've gotta try something else.

The next day Charlene emerges from the basement, she isn't the bubbly person that she was the day before she is grumpy and aggravated, I didn't think that this would be a good time to try to talk to her, grandma made her food she complained about how it tasted, she complained that the coffee was instant, nothing seemed to please her, I saw grandma jumping thru hoops to satisfy her and nothing that she did made a difference to Charlene, it made me happy to see grandma not be in charge, Charlene has taken her power just like she took mine. I knew that my plan of joining forces with Charlene wasn't going to happen at all, but I took pleasure in knowing that she was a one-man wrecking crew and she kept grandma on pins and needles which was good enough for me.

CHAPTER 20

Thanksgiving

Thanksgiving day, everyone is at grandma house eating, drinking and having a good time, it's a good day, I'm having a good time playing with my cousins, as the night progresses it starts to snow us kids are excited looking out of the window waiting for it to stick, making plans to make snow balls the next day, when all of a sudden we heard this big commotion, the grown-ups were fighting, couldn't tell who it was or why but all of us kids were standing by watching, they were tearing up the dining room, it was scary sounded like a heard of horses running thru the house, when the smoke cleared and they were able to separate the fighters it was apparent that I had something to do with the fight, because one of my grandma older goons who I didn't know that well grabbed me up walked out of the front door and thru me down the stairs as I was propelling thru the air I called Jesus, Jesus, please catch me, as I slammed to the ground, I'm lying there, hurting, hurting everywhere too much pain to identify the actual source of the pain, its cold and the snow is falling on me, my grandma is calling my name, "Trina get up" I'm trying but I don't answer her, she walks down the stairs snatches me up, I know now that it's my arm that is hurt, she says where are you hurt I say my arm she tells me to go back into the house, the goon that thru me down the stairs, he's drunk, he leaves with his girlfriend no one says anything, for hours I'm in pain crying and telling her that my arm hurts eventually she takes me to the hospital, my grandma is briefing me on the walk to the hospital that if they asked me what happened I need to tell them that I fell down the stairs trying to play in the snow. When we arrive at the emergency room they take us back to a room and the nurse says what happened sweetie like an idiot I told her the script, I said I fell down the stairs, and the nurse says how did that happen I say we were playing in the snow and I slipped, then grandma joined in saying how clumsy I was and how I was so excited to play in the snow, they believed her. While we were waiting in the ER, my dad showed up, they let him back to the exam room where we were, and he says what happened, before I could say something, grandma went with the falling in the snow story, I just held my head down and looked at the floor, he said Trina what happened I said I fell in the snow never once looking up at him, I couldn't trust him to tell him the truth, I didn't want to make things worse. I had a broken collar bone, they fixed me up and said that I could go home. I just couldn't believe that they believed her, they believed her.

When they got ready to discharge me, daddy asked grandma if we had a ride, she said no that we had walked to the hospital, and daddy said you walked? You made her walk while she was in pain, grandma said we don't live that far plus I didn't have anyone available to take us, Daddy's nostrils started flaring, he was getting upset. The nurse comes in, she says you guys are all set, she went over the prescription and what to expect, daddy interrupted and said, could this injury happen from a fall? She is only 4 feet tall, how could she fall so hard to break her collar bone, she isn't that far from the ground, the nurse says you would be surprised children fall and break their bones every day. Another grown-up that I couldn't trust.

The Court House

Grandma had gotten a letter that stated that she and I needed to appear in court, she and I walked to Sears and Roebuck's it was a department store, she brought me a nice outfit, she was very nice that day, we stopped at the counter where they sold gourmet candies and nuts, she brought a pound of Spanish peanuts and a pound of orange slices, she let me eat some on our walk back home, I wished that she could have been nice like that always. Once we made it back to the house she sat down with me and had me read a few paragraphs from my English book, she told me how well I read, I was in complete shock because before this day I can't recall her ever saying anything nice to me.

The next morning, we got up and caught the bus down to the court house all the way there I'm given instructions on what to say, when we get there I see daddy in the hallway he is with his mom, my other grandma who I label as my nice grandma, they hug me and speak to my mean grandma we all walk into the courtroom, I sit with my dad my nice grandma, my mean grandma sits alone on the other side. They call my dad's name he gets up and he speaks with the judge who asks him for papers and asks him if he has done everything that was asked of him, daddy said yes, they spoke to my mean grandma, and they never said a word to me, I didn't understand what was happening, When it was over my dad offered grandma a ride she declined she said that she had a stop to make and that she didn't want to inconvenience him, I think that she was mad about something that must have been said at the courthouse. She and I walked to the bus stop she was different, I was really scared, I didn't know what would happen to me, what this different mood meant for me, as we approached the house my bladder had gotten so full, so full that I couldn't hold it, I peed myself but I kept walking, it was only when grandma saw the smoke coming from my pants that she had noticed that I had soiled myself she asked me the obvious question did you pee on yourself? and I said yes, she said why, I said that I didn't know, it was cold outside and I was freezing but we kept walking she spoke calmly, she didn't hit me, and when we got to the house she ran some bath water and told me to take a bath, she never hit me, she never yelled, now I'm so scared I can't take it, I wanted it to be over with already, I got out of the bath I waited patiently, I swear that I went to pee more than ten times within the hour I couldn't understand where this pee was coming from, I hadn't had anything to drink. I retreated to my closet and started my usual conversation with Jesus, only this day it was different, Jesus answered me he said that it's over now, I don't know if it was a thought or if I heard his voice, I just know that he said it's over now. I sat there and I called out to him again and asked him more and more questions he didn't respond. I didn't understand why I couldn't hold an actual conversation with him, well a conversation where the both of us are talking together.

CHAPTER 22

The Wait

School is almost over, I'll be going to the 4th grade the upcoming school year, and I'm pretty excited about it, thru all of the drama I never failed a grade, now I'm not saying that I didn't get a bunch of red flags, and plenty of beatings behind those but I guess that it wasn't enough to hold me back.

Settle down the teacher says, we kids are excited were going on a field trip, I don't think that I've ever gone on a field trip, we're going to the Museum of Science and Industry, I don't know what we're going to learn there but never the less I'm excited, the teacher goes on and on about how much the trip cost and that we must bring a bag lunch, all the kids are talking about what they are gonna bring for lunch that day it's a pretty big deal for us, the teacher passes out the permission slips, they have been taken home and signed by our parents or guardians and brought back with $3.oo, I carefully fold my form up and put it in my book bag, before were released from school I check to make sure that it's still there on the walk home from school I tell my cousins that were going on a field trip, they began to share stories of when they went on a trip everyone was so excited, I almost forgot that I was on my way home from school panic hadn't set in, it's a good day, when we get to the house I'm trying to be cool, blend in, I don't want no problems, trying to figure out when it would be a good time to tell grandma about the field trip and ask her if I could go, before

I could do that one of my cousins blurted out, grandma Trina's classroom is going on a field trip, grandma says oh yea where you going Trina, I say they are taking the class to the Museum of Science and Industry, in two weeks and its only $3.00 can I go, grandma says did they give you a permission slip I say yes it's in my book bag, I'll get it and I run off to get the slip, I'm thinking this is going pretty darn smooth, and I'm loving it, I haven't been hit since we went to the court house, I don't know what they said to her but boy was I glad.

Here you go grandma as I hand her the permission slip, she reads it and I'm standing waiting for her to say something she says ok, put this paper on my dresser ill sign it and send it back, so I say, so I can go?, grandma says yes and walks away, it's too good to be true I can't accept that, I need her to call me a name or to yell or to throw something or to curse, to do anything but be nice, she must be losing her mind, I think why is she nice what's going on? Full panic sets in I'm going crazy I retreat to the closet, I don't like it when she hits me or says mean things but I'm used to it, it feels weird when she doesn't do it, am I crazy? I should be happy.

Boxing Ring

Daddy calls me, we talk on the phone, I tell him all about the field trip he is excited too, daddy always seemed to be excited when I told him something, I'm getting older now and I think that he wasn't excited but pretending to be because I was, that was ok with me either way. Daddy says I'm coming to pick you up this weekend that was music to my ears I loved going away with daddy even if he did just take me to my grandma his mother's house and drop me off, I didn't mind, as long as I got away from this house, when we were done talking he says let me speak to Ms. Millie I say ok, I call out, grandma as I put the phone down and was about to run off to find her but as soon as I turned around she was standing there, I look up at her and say my daddy wants to talk to you, she reaches out for the phone, I flinch, she just shakes her head and the whole while she is talking to daddy she is giving me the evil eye, I'm thinking here we go.

I just stand there until she's off the phone, waiting to see what's going to happen I suppose. But she hangs up and says he is gonna pick you up after school tomorrow, I'm so happy I try to not let it show, I say ok and go into the living room where the other children are playing, the girls were playing jacks on the floor can I play I asked? So I'm waiting there for someone to miss so that I can play when grandma walks in the living room, she says Trina what was David talking about, umm nothing really, I was telling him about the field trip, and stuff, she says what about it, I say just where we are going and if I can have money to buy stuff when I'm there, What kind of stuff? She says, Ummm I don't know what they will have I just want money just in case there is something for me to buy, she doesn't say anything else she just sits there watching the tv.

While it seemed that grandma had taken a hiatus on kicking my butt, the constant fights with my cousins hadn't I knew that by engaging in a game of jack's that a fight might ensue but hey that's how we lived, I used those fights as ways to work off the frustration that grandma kept me under. Because I'm winning at the jack's my cousin decides that she doesn't want to play anymore they are her jack's so the game is over, I say you're a sore loser and she starts with the name calling just like she hears grandma do, the only difference is she ain't grandma so I can talk back to her, she says and your black and ugly and I say that's why you have a big apple head and she says that's why yo mama is dead and I say that's why you don't know who yo daddy is, she says, say it again and I'm gonna kick your butt I say that's why you have no daddy and I'm not scared of you, she says you better shut up with your baldheaded butt, I say make me with your bucked teeth butt, she hauls off and slaps me and the fight is on, we are fighting like two caged animals, scratching, biting whatever we can do to win the fight at this time grandma breaks up the fight, she screaming mostly at me, you wanna fight? she's screaming, ok you wanna fight? come on y'all fight she pushes us together we start fighting again, now all of the other kids are standing around us, it's like we are in a makeshift boxing ring, she starts chanting fight, fight, fight till you die, we are fighting literately trying to kill each other with our bare hands, the other children join in on the chanting fight, fight, fight till you die. So we fight, then finally after a few minutes pass grandma breaks up the fight, just when I think it's over she tells one of my other cousins to fight me, so I'm fighting her, she is the sister of the cousin that I was fighting with first, she is younger but the fight is just as intense when she sees that I haven't been defeated she breaks up the fight with the two of us, and send in their brother to fight me now, were fighting and they are still chanting fight, fight, fight till you die and laughing,

I'm crying because I don't want to fight anymore but I have too, then at her command the two sisters jump back into the fight, now all three of them jump me and finally I'm defeated laying on the floor crying I look up to see her with this smile on her face. I get up and run into the closet, this time I don't ask Jesus to kill me I ask him to kill her instead and of course, he didn't.

CHAPTER 24

Weekend Visit With Daddy

Daddy shows up at 5 pm sharp on Friday afternoon, I had been waiting by the window since 3, waiting and watching for his blue Cadillac, He named her Misty blue, daddy loved his car he spent most of Saturday morning washing and waxing her. When I see him turn the corner, I take off to grandma's room to get my bag, I say grandma my daddy's here, and she says OK, take it easy, acting as if you ain't never been anywhere. I stop running immediately but start to speed walking towards the door, I open the door just as daddy is walking up the stairs I break out the door screaming daddy as I run to him, he picks me up and says hey missy, I hug his neck as tight as I can. By this time grandma is at the door with my bag, daddy says how do you do Ms. Millie grandma says I can't complain, yea I hear that daddy says, ok well is that her bag? Grandma says yea he reaches out for it and says alright were gonna get out of here will bring her back round this time on Sunday, before grandma could respond he says missy tell your grandma bye, I say bye grandma she says David put that girl down she ain't hardly a baby, daddy says well she's always gonna be my baby I'm gonna carry her till I can't carry her anymore, grandma just stood there with a scowl on her face, daddy puts me in the car and I don't even look back towards the porch I do not want to see her face again daddy walks around gets in the car, starts it up, he hits the horn before he pulls off and waves his hand, I never look towards the porch as we pull away.

I want to tell daddy about how she made them jump on me the other day but I know that he is a hot head he will go and tell her what I said, not to purposely get me into trouble but to think that he is making things better by talking to her, but I learned from experience that his talking to her only makes things worst so I talk about the field trip instead. Daddy I'm going to need to take a bag lunch to the trip, but we never have food at grandma's house, he stated laughing I know that there ain't no food over there all of those people up in there, I'll bring you a bag lunch and daddy will make it himself. We pull up to daddy's apartment it's a nice brick building seems like it's quiet, we go inside were eating when someone knocks on the back door, it's one of daddy's friends, daddy says come on in man, you know my little girl he says man ain't no denying that one she is a spitting image of you what's her name, daddy said Katrina Denise, my one and only baby, his friend says you should have named Davlena, I start laughing and says excuse me but that's not cute, and we all laugh, daddy says what's up man, come in here let me talk with you, missy finish your food, I Say ok he and the guy go into the living room to talk.

Later on, that night daddy says Missy daddy is gonna bend a few corners gonna take you to mama's house the kids are there I say ok, I knew what this meant, Daddy would drop me off at my nice grandma's house and that's where I would be for the rest of the weekend, but it's was ok with me, daddy showered, shaved and got all dressed up we got into the car and he dropped me off to grandma's house just like I knew that he would. I had plenty of cousins there too but we didn't fight like savages or name call we were just normal kids, we spent our time playing make-believe games in the backyard, my grandpa had a boat we would pretend that we were sailing, and we always had a good time not to mention that grandpa and his friends always had some kind of meat on the grill and he made sure that we ate.

The next day daddy came by with a bag full of zoo-zoos that's what he called junk food, he brought enough chips and candy for all of us kids, he hung around and talked with my grandma for a while the whole time I'm sitting in his lap, I wanted so much for him to take me with him even if it was just back to his place, I just wanted to be with him, but as usual, he would say daddy is gonna bend a few corners I'll be back after a while, and I wouldn't see him till the next day.

CHAPTER 25

Sunday

Sundays at my nice grandma's house were like holidays all of her kids and their kids would be there, grandma would always cook a big meal, we would eat until we were full, the kids would be running and playing, and everyone got along, especially the adults, there was no fighting or arguing It was a different vibe on this side of my family.

As the day begins to wind down a heaviness of sadness drapes me, it consumes me I can barely breathe, I know in a few short hours I will be back in the center of dysfunction, and there is nothing that I can do about it. Before long just as I feared daddy said Missy get your things together daddy is gonna take you home before it gets too late, I feel the lump in my throat begin to form as I said ok, I feel like someone just punched me in the stomach and left a left hollow hole, I make my way up the stairs to grab my bag, it was only 21 stairs but I would walk so slow that it would take a full 5 minutes to get up and another five minutes to come back down, I counted those steps going up and coming down, trying to get my mind off of having to go back, couldn't call it home because it didn't feel like home it felt like a modern-day torture chamber, and no one saw that but me.

I grab my bag and head back down the stairs, the stairway was split, there were 4 stairs, then a landing that had a window, and the last 17 stairs that lead down to the foyer where there was a door to grandma's house and to upstairs and to the front door that leads to the enclosed porch which practically wrapped around half the house, then the exterior door. I decided to sit on the last step right before the landing, you see it was kinda a hiding spot, if daddy would come to the door and call me he couldn't see me sitting there, so I sat there steadily wasting time hoping that daddy would get distracted and forget to call for me, no such luck, Trina lets go daddy yelled, I kick my feet, swing punches in the air, before controlling my tone and say ok daddy I'm coming. For some reason, the fear and pain fell heavy on me, I was dreading going, and I guess that my patience was running thin, I used to be so brave, I knew what was going to happen and I would usually psych myself out just enough that the fear wouldn't overtake me but today was different, I couldn't control it, so I walk down the stairs telling myself you can do it, you've done it before.

Daddy, I'm ready, he says ok go and give grandma and grandpa a hug and kiss, ok I say as I walk into the kitchen I say excuse me, grandma, she was talking to one of my uncles, I say I'm leaving to go home, only the word home came out like a whisper she notices and said what's wrong I say nothing as the lump in my throat feels like it's going to come flying out if I open my mouth wide enough, she says it doesn't look like nothing, then she says come here and she puts me in her lap, she says whatever it is it's gonna be alright ok? I shake my head to motion yes, she says to use your words I say yes ma'am, she kisses me on my cheek and hugs me she starts to laugh and says girl you look just like your daddy should have been a boy, I put on a fake smile as I hop down she pats me on the butt and say have a good week at school, I say ok, where is granddaddy he is in the room she says, I go to the bedroom door, I knock and say granddaddy while pushing the door open he is sitting in his recliner chair he says to come in Tinee, that's what he called me, I said I'm leaving I just wanted to hug you goodbye, he says alright as he gets up from the chair, I hug him around his legs as my head rest on his tummy he pats my back and he says to be a good girl, I say ok, he kisses me in the top of my head I turn and walk out of the room. Everyone says by, and daddy and I get in the car, I sit there quiet, daddy says missy don't start this you are a big girl you're not a baby anymore, I say yes sir he says why don't you wanna go back there, I really can't tell him because he will only make it worst, so I say I just wanna stay with you daddy, he says you know that daddy is working on that and in the meantime, we have to do what's right, it won't be long now. Daddy not knowing what to do says do you have any money? I say No, he says "Missy daddy told you to never spend all of your money you should always keep at least a dollar in your pocket", I say ok, and he reaches in his pocket and gives me a $20 bill he says spend one dollar a day and when you get down to $6 daddy will give you some more, daddy didn't understand that I wasn't motivated by money or things I just wanted him, sometimes I felt like that I was a burden to daddy, I knew that he loved me but I felt like he was just to busy to be bothered with an ugly, skinny, bald headed little girl, he of course never called me those names but I knew that's what I was because those words were used to describe me, the girl without a mother, the girl who didn't belong, the ugly, skinny, baldheaded little girl that should have been a boy, yep that who I was!!!!!!

I take the money and I see that we are not far from the house my nerves are bad, I have this pressing urge to pee, my legs start shaking and my hands are clammy, we pull up to the house daddy is parking the car, he says let's do it fluid, he was always saying some cute little statement, I sit there, no smiles no giggles, I sit there he looks at me and I can tell that he was not in the mood for my foolishness tonight but I didn't care, I sit there, he says Katrina Denise not tonight, I sit there he reaches in the back seat he grabs my bag, he gets out walks around the car, by this time grandma is on the porch she says how you, slang for how are you, daddy say just fine, he opens the door and says come on, I sit there and he kneels down to look me in the face and says baby please don't do this, I lock my eyes on his hoping that he will see the desperation in my eyes but he doesn't, instead he says baby girl come on now don't do this, I sit there he says daddy will give you whatever you want if you would just get out of the car, I sit there, he says, I'll buy you a puppy, me nothing, he says I'll take you shopping, me nothing, he says Ill but you a bike, I turn my heads towards him and say, what kind he says what do you want I say a pink huffy, he says with a banana seat I say yes, he says It's yours I say when,he says tomorrow, I say you promise, he says I promise just as I'm about the get out of the car I hear the wicked witch that is grandma yelling with that high pitched voice Trina get your butt out of that car, she had made her way down to the car she heard the whole conversation, she says David you ain't got to bribe her, get your but out of that car, daddy says no its alright Ms. Millie this is just something that we do, I look up and I see the scowl on her face and I know that I'm getting it for sure now, so I turn my head back towards the windshield I'm not going, things escalate quickly, after a few minutes of daddy trying to talk me out of the car, and grandma talking over him he decides that he is going to pick me up out of the car, I'm kicking screaming bloody murder he is pulling me and I'm trying to grab ahold of the car door, anything that I can grab which will keep him from getting me out of the car, I lose he is carrying me up the stairs and I'm screaming no, no, no daddy don't leave me here, grandma is still talking Daddy is upset he says to grandma Ms. Millie what is going on over here that this child don't wanna be here as he's fighting to keep a hold of me at this time, I'm thinking I'm not staying here when he lets me down I'm running, grandma says I don't know what's wrong with her, and I scream your gonna beat me, your gonna starve me your gonna make them fight me, daddy please don't leave me, grandma stops talking daddy says wait a minute what is going on? I say it again, grandma is still standing there, daddy looks confused, but I can tell that he is mad because his nostrils have flared, but the million-dollar question is what is he going to do?

He says excuse me Ms. Millie can I talk to Katrina alone please grandma says Trina don't you start that lying, David you don't know how this child lies, daddy says ok but do you mind, she went back on the porch, Daddy says ok what is going on? I say it's true daddy but I can't tell you because you always tell her what I said then when you leave I get it worse, I tell him everything, about the name calling, the fighting with the other kids the beatings the starvation, the almost drowning, the burns, the truancy officer, how they killed queenie, the closet, the creamed corn and how I want to DIE. I tell, everything daddy just sits there, he tells me to get back in the car I'm happy, as he is walking up the stairs, he looks like me when I'm walking the stairs at my grandma's house to get my things like he is dreading what's about to happen. Grandma and her goons are standing there daddy says to Ms. Millie with respect and in a very calm voice, can I take Trina back with me tonight, with everything that's going on, it will probably be the best thing, emotions are high and a lot of things have been said, this will give everyone a time to cool off, ill drop her off to school in the morning before he could finish talking the police pull up, grandma had called the police, I'm sitting in the car looking, I'm really scared now, they walk up the stairs, I get out of the car to go stand by daddy, one the officer says what's the problem, ma'am? grandma says David what's the problem? Daddy said we don't have a problem officer I'm just asking her if I could keep my daughter another night, the grandma who has her temporary guardian papers in hand says you get every other weekend and you are supposed to return her by 8 pm its almost 9 p.m. now your late as it is, daddy throws his head back in unbelief, he says Millie I wasn't late, and I understand that I have her every other weekend I'm just asking, grandma starts yelling who do you think you are? The other officer says ok, ok, calm down, Sir, can you come down here to talk with me, as daddy and I were walking down the stairs to talk to the officer grandma is yelling my name Trina, Trina get back up here, I keep walking. The other officer is telling her just relax what's going on? Grandma goes on to say how daddy was late and how he thinks he can do what he wants, she is going on and on with her exaggerated lies as usual.

Daddy says to the officer I don't know what's going on but every time I have to bring my daughter back she gets really sad, I didn't think much of it, you know thinking she is just being a kid, but tonight I had to physically tear her from the car and thru all of the commotion she made some serious accusations, the officer said like what? He is writing on his notepad, he never looks up, Daddy said to tell him, missy, I said grandma is always mean to me she calls me names and curses at me, she threatens to put me six feet under, the officer's look's up and says what? Where? I say six feet under like in a grave like my mother, I say she won't let me eat sometimes and she hits me, chokes me, and throws me around. The officer takes off his hat he says did you know this sir? Daddy said no not exactly, he says Katrina had told me a time or two about getting hit and when I questioned Ms. Millie she assured me that she was just disciplining her nothing more than that, but after those few times Katrina never said anything more, now he is standing looking like a deer in stuck in headlights, his wheels are turning he finally gets it. The officer said stay here, he calls the officer down the stairs and they start talking, grandma now starts yelling again,

Trina look at this mess you have caused, Daddy says Millie don't do that, then officer that had been talking to daddy and me, he said while pointing to grandma don't talk to them and then pointing to daddy you don't respond to them, we all just stood there, but grandma was continually talking but to her goons.

CHAPTER 26

The Police

The police officers called their supervisor who shows up on the scene he gets out of the car and talks with the officers then he walks over to daddy and I, daddy had opened the car door I'm sitting in the front seat and he is leaning up against the car, as the supervisor approaches daddy stand up straight, the supervisor extends his hand and introduces himself daddy, reaches out his hand states his name and the officer says Sir this is a civil matter and there isn't really much that we can do, the child looks healthy and doesn't appear to have any bruises, but I do understand your concern and if I were you I would have called the authorities as well, daddy interrupted and said I didn't call Sir, Ms. Millie called, long before I had asked her if I could keep my daughter another night, that says to me that she is guilty of everything that this child says, the supervisor says oh wow, well yes that changes things, he says hold on and he goes up to speak to grandma, who says that she called the police because she knew that my dad was going to want to keep me by the way that I was acting. The supervisor asked her why she felt that way. If he had ever done that before, grandma said no but he has the nerve to question me about what goes on in my god damn house, hmmm, the supervisor said, and asks grandma who is the social work that is assigned to this case. Grandma says I know nothing bout no social worker and hands him the paperwork, all I know is that I am her grandma, that's my dead daughter's child I know that for sure, then you got this man, I know nothing bout him talking about he's her daddy, hell if you feed a dog long enough it will look like you, The supervisor says ok Ma'am that's enough as he reads the documents and notices that there hadn't been a social worker assigned, the supervisor says hold tight, he walks back down to his car called someone on his radio, he spoke with the other officers briefly and asked grandma to come down the stairs at this time her goons go crazy the entire time they had been quiet, they are now yelling and asking, come down there for what? Y'all ain't gonna arrest my mama, because Trina is lying! the officers tell them to settle down no need for anybody to go to jail tonight especially you two for disorderly conduct, do you understand? They don't exactly stop talking just bring it down a few notches, grandma's mind is so twisted it brought a smile to her face to see her goons standing up to defend her in her wrongdoing. As grandma walked down the stairs with this smirk on her face she was looking at me trying to intimidate me I just drop my head, I don't want to see her ugly old face, daddy squeezes my hand. The supervisor says ma'am this child has stated some serious allegations and to keep the peace we are going to let her father take her with him tonight, a social worker will be here in the morning to speak with you and she will make the call on what happens next, he then says Sir you may leave and take your daughter with you, you must take her to school in the morning a social worker will come to her school to speak with the both of you. Grandma isn't happy and she begins by yelling and raising hell as she does so well. The supervisor who just wasn't having any of that FOOLISHNESS told her matter of factly to shut up and go inside and if it took her too long to do so she would be spending the night in jail. I must have a twisted mind as well because seeing someone bully the bully gave me great pleasure, I wanted to yell out nanny, nanny boo-boo, who's scared now but I guess that I knew better, I jumped in the car with daddy and we pulled off.

CHAPTER 27

The Social Worker

Daddy is trying to do my hair, I can't stop laughing he looks so serious, he doesn't have any hair grease he says hold on a minute he comes back with Vaseline he says this will work, he takes a big glob and rubs it in his hands, as it starts to melt he rubs it all over my hair then he brushes it back and make a ponytail, only it looks more like a pigtail, I say daddy it's not long enough to make a ponytail so you have to wrap it around so that it looks like a ball then put another rubber band on to secure it, he says let me think, I don't think that I have another rubber band then, he says wait let's see if they have thrown the paper yet, he goes on the front porch comes back in yelling B-I-N-G-O, got one as he laughs he thinks that he is so clever, I laugh with him and he wraps the rubber band around the hair and secures it. I say let me see as I run to the bathroom he follows behind me as I look in the mirror, not bad, not bad for a first timer I say, daddy says first time, not me I've done this a few times, I have six sisters I know a little something, I stand there looking at myself in the mirror, he is standing in the doorway of the bathroom watching me watch myself, I say daddy why am I ugly? He walks into the bathroom and sits on the bathtub he turns me around to face him and he says you are not ugly, there is nothing ugly about you, you are fearfully and wonderfully made, god made you in his image and he made you look like me only cuter, I can see your mother in you also and she was a very beautiful woman, promise me something

Missy, I say yes, he says don't ever keep anything from daddy, no matter what it is or no matter what somebody tells you that they will do to you if you tell me, I realize now where I messed up but going forward for the rest of my life I will never let anybody hurt you again, please baby girl give daddy another chance, we both with tears in our eyes stare at each other. I say ok daddy I promise to never keep anything else from you.

Daddy and I pull up to the school, we get out of the car and are walking to the school I feel like a million bucks I'm happy, I see some of my classmates they are staring, usually when your parent comes to school that means that you've done something very good, or are in trouble. We go into the building daddy says where is the office I point and daddy says to use your words, I say yes Sir it's around this corner we walked around the corner and up to the door, Daddy opens the door the woman behind the counter says can I help you, Daddy says my name is David Sprawls and my daughter is a student here, we are supposed to meet with a social worker this morning, the woman says ok, please have a seat, she goes into the principal's office, his name is Mr. Hall he was very well respected by his entire staff and us kids had a healthy fear of him. Mr. Hall came out and said Mr. Wade, it's a pleasure to meet you, sir, Daddy said good morning Sir, but I'm not Mr. Wade my daughter is carrying her mother's name, my name is Sprawls as he extends his hands, how are you? Mr. Hall says I apologize, please come this way, Daddy says no harm no foul as we walk into the principal's office, Mr. Hall says I don't have all of the details of this situation as of yet but first we are going to have you all sit with our school social worker to get us caught up, do you mind if I sit in? Daddy says no of course not, Mr. Hall picks up his phone and calls for the social worker, her name was Ms. Maddox, I had seen her around the school but had never had any interactions with her, when she walked into the office she introduced herself and began by asking daddy what was going on. Daddy told of how I acted upon being dropped off and the situation that followed, Ms. Maddox said Katrina can you tell me about what goes on at home, I told her all about everything as she was taking notes, every so often she would look up from notes and our eyes would lock, she would look so sad, I wanted to just hug her, although she was feeling sad for me. The social worker from the state shows up her name was Mrs., Belinsky, she was a white woman, she was tall and very thin, her hair was long and looked like it felt like silk, I never really saw white people, there were only a few of them that worked in our school, and I didn't know what to think about her, should I be afraid? Would she be nice? I didn't know anything about white people, I just knew that my dad spoke differently around them, as he did with the police the night before. Mrs. Belinsky introduced herself, she talked with my dad and the other grownups first, then she turned to me and she said Hello Ms. Katrina, I giggled because she called me Ms.Katrina, Then I said hello, I was going to change the way I spoke too because that's what dad had done, she says can I call you Karina I was about to shake my head but I remember daddy always said use your words so I said yes ma'am, she said ok great and you can call me Mrs. B if you can't pronounce my name, I said yes Ma'am again, she smiled and looked up at daddy and said she's too cute, and you guys look like twins, I had never heard anyone refer to me as being cute, huh, wonder if that's true or was she just being nice. Mrs. B, says so I understand that someone has hurt you. I say yes ma'am, can you tell me who she says? I say, grandma, can you tell me what she did? I say yes, well she likes to slap me, sometimes choke me, sometimes she doesn't let me eat, and she always says mean things to me, and, Mrs. B says slow down sweetie can you tell me about when she chokes you, I say well there were many times but the last time was when I had just come back from my daddy's house for the weekend visit, umm-hmm says Mrs. B. I continued and said, she asked me if he had given me some money, I said yes then she said let grandma have it so that she can buy you all some ice cream, I gave her the money and she sent to the store for the ice cream and she told them to get coffee and some snuff too, so I said grandma please don't spend it all and she got mad and said that my mouth was to smart then she slapped me the floor while I was on the floor crying she was talking about having to reprogram me every time I go to those people house, I jumped up and tried to run because I knew what was about to happen but she grabbed me by my shirt, she spun me around, she began to twist the shirt right under my chin until it was chocking me, Mrs. B said Katrina you said the last time? how often does she choke you, I don't know but a lot, as I was gonna continue talking Mrs. B says that enough sweetheart. She asked Mr. Hall if he would leave the office that she needed to undress me and look at my body for scars, she asked daddy if he felt comfortable with staying he said yes. Mr. Hall stood up and walked from around his desk, he looked at me with so much compassion in his eyes, I think that he needs a hug too, he says as he leaves the office I'll be right out here when you're done but take your time. Katrina, I'm going to need you to take off all of your clothes but leave on your underwear ok? she says, yes ma'am I said as I undressed, she further went on to explain that she was needing to take pictures of me also. She did her examination and told daddy that she was gonna have to go speak with my grandmother and the judge that is already working on the case and because there are no physical signs of abuse other than a few scars that are already healed and could be discounted as normal because children are always falling she went on further to say that, Katrina doesn't look like she's being starved either so more than likely she will have to stay with her grandmother for another few days maybe even weeks, Daddy's face tightened up but he didn't say anything, then Mrs. B, put her hand on top of daddy's hand and said I believe her, I can hear the pain in her voice, I hope that this will give you some comfort, I will speak to the judge and see about expediting his ruling, you have done everything that has been asked of you. Mr.Sprawls do you believe in God, Daddy said yes I do, she says well keep praying, prayer changes things.

As of now, Katrina will have to go back to her Grandma's house today after school until we can get this matter taken care of, I'm headed to the house now and I will let her know to keep her hands and mouth off of this child. I will be doing an unannounced home visit every day until it's resolved and Ms. Maddox will visit with Katrina during the school week daily to make sure no new abuse occurs and to make sure that has eaten.

Daddy stood up thanked the ladies and shook their hands, Mrs. B says we will give you all a moment please meet us in the main lobby I'll get copies for you. Daddy said, of course, the women left and closed the door, Daddy said baby girl I'm sorry but this is the way that it has to be for now. But if she does or says anything to hurt you, you tell me or the social worker ok? I say ok and I hug daddy's neck, daddy I'm really scared I said to him and so am I daddy said, but I have an idea. Come on, we walk out of the office and daddy says Mrs. B, would it be ok If I went over every evening after work, I won't cause any problems I just need to see her every day, Mrs. B says absolutely, and I will let the grandmother know that you will be stopping by. Thank you so very much daddy said, then he says, I'm going to walk her to class and I will stop back by her to get the paperwork, as were going up to the classroom, daddy is coaching me on how to behave and not to upset grandma when I get home today after school, I'll be over there this evening too when I get home from work, I say ok. Daddy knocks on the classroom door the teacher Mrs. Frazier comes to the door and she says Katrina we missed you this morning are you ok? I say yes ma'am go on to your seat get your math book out and turn to page thirty-two, ugh, I think to myself I hate math we should stay in the office a little while longer, I say bye daddy I had fun with you this morning, he says I had fun with you too, I will see you later, you got money I say yes and go into the classroom. Daddy says to Mrs. Frazier, I'm sorry to interrupt, Mrs. Frazier said it's ok I've been informed of the situation she says I should have known, this poor girl, she comes to school every day with such sad eyes, she doesn't have the best clothes but she is always clean, a few hours in she perks up but then around 2 pm she falls back into a slump, I'm trained to recognize these things, please forgive me. Daddy says, of course, Mrs. Frazier says I even joked with her once about how she eats everything on her tray, I just assumed that she was a healthy eater, I felt so bad when I found out. Daddy says well don't beat yourself up about it she is so brave she handled this all by herself, but I wanted to give you my work and home phone number, if you see anything or if Katrina seems different please don't hesitate to call me, Mrs. Frazier walked into the classroom to get a pen and paper, she said children we have a visitor we must be on our best behavior all of the class responded with yes Mrs. Frazier, she goes back to the hallway and takes down my father's information.

That was a busy day for me, I was called to the office over 5 times talking to this one, and that one, it hardly did no school work and that was ok with me.

CHAPTER 28

The Pink Huffy

Walking home from school that day my cousins had tons of questions about what had happened the night before, not being able to trust them I just said that I was crying and wanted to stay at my dad's house, that he and grandma had disagreed and the police were called but everything was ok now. As we approached the house my legs felt like they were gonna crumble into a million pieces I wish that they would have, that old familiar lump in the throat and hollow stomach were back, grandma was on the porch as all the kids run up the stairs I just walk with my head hung low, she says ohh Trina look at this mess you've caused, I didn't say anything she says you hear me talking to you, I say Hi grandma, hi grandma that all that you can say? She asks, I said yes ma'am, she said to get in there and take them clothes off, are they new? She asks, I say yes, oh y'all had this planned, there was no store open for y'all to be shopping last night, I say no grandma we didn't daddy has things for me at his house, oh excuse me little miss proper T-H-I-N-G-S as she sings the word while rolling her neck, you thank you too much just like those folk as she grabs my arm and gives me a push towards the front door, once inside I felt like everybody was looking at me, I went to change clothes and retreated to the closet. I stayed there until I heard my daddy's voice I, swung the closet door open screaming daddy he says hey baby girl, grandma says hello David, she was trying to be nice but you can see it all in her face, she wanted to scratch his eyes out, he says hello, come on outside Trina, daddy has something for you when I got out to the porch I could see the handlebars thru the window, I said a bike you got it daddy, as I was running to the car, daddy said I promised you that I would get it, I said I know but I didn't get out of the car and we both started laughing, he opens the back door and pulls the bike out, it was a pink huffy with a white banana seat, it had pink and white tassels hanging from the handlebars, it was beautiful, I was so excited, daddy said wait a minute can you ride a bike,? yes, I can I screamed, that was a lie I had never been on a bike before, but I wasn't going to let him take that beauty back.

Daddy said hop on then, I jumped on and started peddling, and crashed into a tree, daddy said I thought that you said that you could ride, I said I will in a few minutes, daddy and I both laughed, and we went into the alley where we had more room daddy and I went up and down the alley, until I was riding that girl by myself, we were having so much fun that I forgot all about my recent drama. Then daddy said ok baby daddy has got to go, but I'll be back tomorrow hearing those words took all of my happiness away when we emerged from the alley and back to the front of the house my grandma and Mary and the kids were sitting on the porch everyone looked like they were mad at me, I didn't want daddy to leave, I was scared for real. Daddy walked up to the porch and said Ms. Millie, do you have a place to keep the bike? Or do I need to take it with me, Grandma said yes, we can keep it in the basement he says ok, I'm gonna get out of here and I will see you tomorrow, grandma just sat there, he walked back down the stairs kissed me on the cheek then whispered in my ear she won't bother you anymore stop looking like your scared. I said but I am scared then tried to smile. Daddy got in the car and left.

When daddy pulled off I took off, I heard grandma calling me to come back here ride to the corner and back when I got back in front of the house she said lets the other kid's ride, you all take turns let everybody get a ride to the corner and back it was so many kids, there needless to say I never rode the bike again that day.

Later that night it was a weird energy in the house, grandma was defeated she stayed in her room the rest of the night, she wasn't raising hell throughout the house like she usually does, it's sad to say but I wish that she was up raising hell and tormenting me, then I would have my normal fear and not this new fear that I could not understand. I was able to eat dinner without incident, it was a normal day but that made me more nervous than I had ever been, right before bed, grandma called my name and a feeling of relief came over me, I was saying finally let's get this over with, I walk into her room expecting to get slapped right back out into the hallway but no she sat on the side of her bed and she said "you may have to go live with your daddy, and I'm thinking yaaaaaaa, she says I don't think that he wants you, he only wants your social security check, I asked what that was, she said it's what the government gives to children after their parents die, I said ok, she said so I have to let you go, you have done already went down there and told them, white folks, all of those lies, they didn't believe you. You ain't did shit you better remember that what goes on in my house stays in my house you better not tell nobody about my business when you leave here, just because you will be over there doesn't mean that I can't get to you, you will still have to come to visit me "I stood there looking at her she said remember queenie", I just stood there she said "answer me" I said yes ma'am. She said don't forget it, now get out of my face.

I walked away excited that I will be leaving, I wanted to ask her when but I didn't want to cause any problems, I had gotten away without getting hit so far, and I wasn't going to push it. A feeling of peace came over me, that crazy urge for her to just hit me already went away, I had no anxiety or nervousness, I felt weird but I liked it. I went back to the closet where I stayed for the rest of the night. I immediately called Jesus, I said thank you for a good day, thank you for letting me go to my dad's house for good.

CHAPTER 29

The Disappearing Bike

Daddy showed up every day like he said he would some days he stayed longer than other days, a few times I would say daddy there is no food and we go off and have dinner, this was like having the best of both worlds. One Friday afternoon I was sitting on the porch waiting for my turn to ride MY bike when daddy pulled up and he said is that your bike that she's on, I said yes, he says why is she ridding and you sitting here, I said because grandma said that we all have to take turns, we used to all ride to the corner and back and trade-off now we all get 30 minutes and I'm up next so I'm waiting, daddy said oh hell no, he walks up to the door and knocks while calling out her name, Ms. Millie as he opens the door, grandma is in the kitchen he walks thru the house, grandma says how you? Daddy says I'm ok, why are Trina sitting on the porch and someone else riding her bike? Grandma said I asked her to share with the other kids because they don't have a bike and it's not fair to them, daddy says I don't care if it's not fair to them, and they aren't my responsibility why can't their daddy buy them a bike? Grandma says well David it's not like that, daddy says look enough is enough I let you take her clothes and give them to the other kids and say nothing about that but you're doing too much now, I brought that bike for my baby and if you ain't gonna let her ride it I'll take it away from here. You don't have to do that she says as she walks towards the front door, she goes to the porch and calls out to my cousin who is riding the bike she says to bring the bike back, Trina's daddy wants nobody riding the bike, my cousin who is just as nasty as my grandma jumps off the bike and let it slam to the ground I look at daddy he shakes his head no, as to tell me not to say anything, he and I go to the alley I ride and he runs alongside me laughing and having a good time when he was about to leave I said daddy how much longer do I have to stay here, he said soon baby soon, we walk back to the front where his car is parked, I asked him if he would help me put the bike away, I know that no one is gonna help me bring it in now.

That night was rough, it seemed as if everyone was mad at me, so to the closet I went, the next day was Saturday I had planned to get up and go for a long ride on my bike, once I had done my chores and was able to go outside I went to the basement to get my bike but could not find it, I went back upstairs and said grandma, I can't find my bike, she says what do you mean you can't find it? It's not in the basement, she says it has to be, she didn't seem to be too concerned, I searched everywhere but could not find the bike, I gave up on looking for it and decided that I would go to the park, one of my cousins who I deemed to be my favorite cousin was in the house watching the Dukes of Hazards on TV, he and I had a special bond we were very close he always showed me empathy, I trusted him and I would tell him when my dad would give me money, and we would sneak off from the other kids and when they would ask where we were going we would say that we were going to take care of business, those were our code words for let's go get snacks and go to the park to eat them, we couldn't let anyone know that I had money, grandma would be sure to take it, after a few times of her taking the money I got smart and would put the dollar bills in my panties, I would always spend up to the dollar to prevent having any change. I walk up to my cousin who was watching tv and say you wanna go take care of business he says yes we take off thru the alley there was a candy store close to the park that we went too. we liked to go a little farther from the house so that we wouldn't get caught, I say while looking at him I'm hungry I didn't eat that rice this morning there was no butter or sugar he says me either, I say I have enough money we can go to jimmy G's we can get a burger or an Italian beef, fries and a pop, we started laughing and running thru the alley towards the restaurant, we like to play like we were spies, we would peep around the buildings looking for grandma goons we didn't want to get caught that would be a beat down for real for me, so we do our spy thing all the way to the restaurant as we get closer I say wait I gotta get the money out of my secret stash, he says where is it, I say in my panties, ewww he says as he laughs, we go into the alley I hide behind the dumpster and pull out the moist dollars, we walk into the restaurant, we ask the cashier how much would it be to get an Italian beef, fries with mild sauce a two grape pops, she says get out of here, I say no we got money she says let me see, I show her a $10 bill she says ok $7.25 I say ok we will take it. Will it be for here or to go, I say here, and can you cut it in half she says do you want me to split the fries too I say yes, thank you. She gives us the soda pop and we sit down, were so happy we feel like real spies we had completed a mission, while we were waiting on the food we devise a story in case we get caught, we decided to say that we went out to find pop bottles and sold them for money, we often did do that so that sounded good.

The cashier calls us to get the food I gave her the $10 bill and told her to keep the coins as a tip and to give me the $2 back we sit down in a booth and began to eat it was delicious when all of a sudden, the door opens and it's one of the goons, he is with one of his friends, he sees us and says what are y'all doing we both were scared we knew that he was gonna go back and tell on us. We were just eating my cousin says, where did y'all get money, he says we sold bottles, y'all had that many bottles, we both say yes, he says let me search you, my cousin said for what, he snatches him up, and start going thru his pockets, I'm scared because I didn't have time to stash the money back in my panties when the cashier yells leave those kids alone, the goon says I'm their uncle, she say then what you searching them for at that time the man who was in the back cooking came out and told him you can't do that up in here, the friend that was with goon said man leave then kids alone they must have been hungry, the goon says sounding like a little girl I'm gonna tell mama on y'all, we start wrapping up what's left of our food, the goon and his friend go to the counter to order something we take off running, we go to our park and sit inside the igloo to finish up, the igloo is open on both ends but no one could see us if we are up against the wall on the inside, I don't know why this park had a igloo in the middle of the sand box but that was our secret spy hide away.

We finish our food, and put together an air-tight story, I say no matter what she does to either of us, we sold the bottles to get the money to buy the food ok, and we put that on a pinky swear. walking home from the park we see this boy that lives around the corner from us, he is in the alley popping wheelies on a bike, he doesn't have a bike, we say Tony whose bike is that? he stops and says my mama brought this bike from your uncle last night, my cousin and I look at each other, it's MY PINK HUFFY, someone tried to spray paint it purple, it was a sloppy paint job, you could still see the pink paint on the metal frame, I'm about to say that's my bike but my cousin grabs my hand as says don't say anything, he says aright we will holla at you later, as we start to walk away I said why didn't you let me say something he said then he would have gone home to tell his mama, just tell your daddy when he comes over.

The Confrontation

That Saturday was wasting away, we had eaten too much we were laying around on the back porch when the goon comes thru the back gate he said I'm about to tell on y'all, we just look up at him and continued laying on the porch, a few minutes later here she comes you can hear those flat feet stomping thru the house, she pushes open the back door, where y'all get money from, we both sat up, I wasn't scared because ever since the police got involved she had learned how to keep her hands to herself, we said in Unison we sold pop bottles, y'all had that many bottles?, we both said yes, we had been finding bottles for a few weeks, I ain't saw no bottles where did you keep them, he said under the porch, we hadn't rehearsed that part of the lie, under the porch, he jumped up and said right here grandma we still have some, she walked down the stairs I followed her, the goon right behind me, he said see, I looked at him, he smiled showing off his dimples, grandma said I ought to beat y'all's ass, ain't no food up in here and y'all at the restaurant and before I knew what was happening I said well he was in there getting food too, while he was telling on us, he looked at me and said I was in there with lil man getting something for his mama, I just rolled my eyes, grandma says where did you get money from, he said I didn't have no money mama you know how she lies, by this time my Aunt Mary was at the back door yelling Trina, I said Ma'am your daddy is here she said, ok I'm screaming as I took off running, I went out to the front porch, Daddy I've been waiting on you all day, daddy says well I'm here now, he says what were you doing? I said grandma was questioning us about where we got money from, daddy nostrils flaring says why? Because we got caught at the restaurant eating, who is we he asked, I pointed to my cousin he said what restaurant, I said Jimmy G's, is that on Madison and Kedzie? daddy asks, yep I said, daddy says that's too far for y'all to be walking too many busy streets, we took the ally's daddy, well cars come thru the alley too, I know but we were hungry, I told you that we never have food, daddy says well I spoke to the social worker today she is just waiting to get the paperwork the judge already signed off on it, you will be going with me any day now, I'm gonna go get a bike for me too so that we can go bike riding together, would you like that? My smile dropped and I said about that, daddy well someone stole my bike and sold it to the boy around the corner, nostril-flaring who stole it? He says, I say one of the goons, he said how do you know, I saw the boy riding on it, they tried to spray paint it purple, he told us that his mama brought it, where does he live, around the corner on congress do you know the house I said yes, come on get in the car, daddy yelled Ms. Millie I'm about to take her to the store we will be right back, grandma was saying something daddy just drove off, we pulled up to the house there was some people on the porch, three ladies, and a man one lady was wearing a purple dress sitting in a chair drinking a RC Cola, another lady wearing a yellow romper, she was braiding a man's hair, there was a younger woman, wearing some red short shorts and a white tube top daddy said you know which one of these ladies is his mama, I said no, but his name is lil tony, we got out of the car, daddy walked up to the porch, he said how are y'all doing this evening, fine and so are you the lady who was wearing the short shorts said as she was smiling from ear to ear, Daddy smiled and said I'm looking for lil Tony's, mama, the lady in the purple said that's my son, what did he do now?, daddy said nothing, he told my daughter that you brought a bike for him from one of Millie boys, yes I did, what's it to you she said, well I believe that the bike that you brought belongs to my daughter daddy said, now that's some bullshit I gave him $35 who gonna give me my motherfuckin money back, daddy said ma'am I didn't come around her for no trouble I just wanna see if the bike is mine, and ill let you and him figure that out, I thought that we could handle this like adults, I didn't want to have to get the police involved, wait police ain't nobody got time for that, how you gonna prove its your bike, what kind of bike is it anyway, it's a brand new pink huffy with a white banana seat, white wall tires and it has pink and white tassels hanging from the handle bars, ha she jumps up from the seat and says the bike is purple, daddy says yes my daughter told me that it was spray painted and that the pink can still be shown underneath the purple paint, well if your daughter know so much how come she left it where somebody can steal it? Daddy says look ma'am are you gonna let me see the bike or no, your son already told us who you brought it from, rather you show it to me or not, your gonna have to explain to the police about buying stolen property, y'all have a good evening, come on Missy, as we were walking away the lady said god dammit wait a minute, she opened the screen door and called Tony, get that bike and bring it round front, tony is yelling something from within the house, Boy get that bike and bring it round here fo I go upside your head, a few seconds later tony came from around the house with the bike, the spray paint job was sloppy at best, everyone could clearly see that the frame was pink, daddy stood there looking at the bike shaking his head saying this don't make any since, just messed up a perfectly good bike, well that's ours for sure, I'm sorry son but I'm gonna be taking this bike back, Tony said aww man, I don't never get nothing, his mother said I'm gonna get you a bike boy, go get my shoes I'm going round there he is gonna give me my money back, bring me that phone, I'm about to call my brother, he is gonna give me my money or he gonna get his ass beat, Daddy said come on baby as he picked up the bike and put it in the car. We drove back around the corner everyone was sitting on the porch, daddy told me I'm gonna take the bike to my house, Daddy will paint it back pink for you, ok thank you, daddy.

We get out of the car, and daddy says Ms. Millie one of your sons sold my baby's bike to a woman around the corner, I went back to get it, and now the woman is round there clowning she wants her money back, How you know my sons sold the bike? Who told you that? You gonna keep on listening to Trina and she gonna get you hurt, Nostril flaring daddy fired back she ain't gonna get me hurt and ain't nobody gonna hurt her no god damn mo, and I mean that try me if you want too, I can't wait till they give me the word to get my kid away from round you, everything got to be her fault she ain't told your boy to steal her bike and sell it, that's what's wrong with them now. Forgive me for cursing, but I've bout had enough of this mess. Grandma didn't say anything, daddy said are you hungry I say yes he says get in the car, I'm about to take my baby to get something to eat I'll bring her right back, she says ain't no food up in there, she lying bout that too?

We pull up to Donald Ducks a local place that served the best Chicago hot dogs and burgers, it was one of those drive-up spots where they bring the food out to the car, we sat in the car and ate, I told daddy about how grandma said that he only wanted me for the social security check, daddy got mad again and said she can keep that pocket change, I'm just done with this all, can't wait till it's over. When we pull back up to grandma's house there was a big commotion, Lil Tony's mom had come around to grandma's house with her brothers and what looked like her entire family looking to get her money back for the bike, the goons weren't home just grandma and the kids, daddy and I just sat in the car and watched, the crowd finally dissipated, and we got out of the car and went into the house, Daddy kissed me goodnight and told me to go to bed Grandma was fuming mad, I went into the closet where I fell asleep.

CHAPTER 31

The Fight

The next day was quiet some us kids went to church with Ms. Bursee she was our neighbor, she often took us to church with her, I didn't particularly like going because they couldn't sing at her church, and it was boring, but It was always better than just sitting in the house, I was super excited that tomorrow would be my field trip and I was gonna have to call daddy to remind him to bring me the bag lunch, once we got home from church I immediately called daddy to remind him of the field trip and to bring the lunch, he says that he didn't forget that he would be there shortly, while waiting on daddy to come, we were sitting on the front porch and decided to play rock teacher, rock teacher was a game, I'm not sure where it came from but we played it a lot, all of us kids would sit on the bottom step and one person would find a rock and put it in his hands, he would present both of his hands in a closed fist, as he would go to each of us and we would have to guess which hand the rock was in, if you guessed right you would advance to the next step which would be the nest grade, until you got to the top, the first person to the top would be the winner. While were playing the game we see what looked like a mob of people coming down the street, it was lil Tony's mother and her family again they were there looking for the goons again, they walk up to the porch and told us to go inside to get them, us kids we were scared so we all ran into the house to get grandma, she says go in the basement and wake up Charlene, one of my cousins went to wake her, the goons are in the alley playing basketball, one of my cousins go out the back door to get them, all of lil Tony's mama and her family was on our porch yelling and cursing, I was really scared, I ran into the closet a few minutes later it sounded like everybody was fighting it was a lot of noise, screaming and just cursing, I came out of the closet and looked out of the window everybody was fighting, Charlene, Mary, the goons, their friends even grandma was hitting people with a stick, I was so scared, I ran to the phone to call my daddy, but for some reason I kept calling the wrong number, when I couldn't get my daddy I just called 911, it was like a scene from a movie there were so many people fighting that I couldn't really see who was doing what, soon I heard the police sirens and the people started running thru the alley, down the street in every direction, so did the goons, Charlene and Mary went in the basement, when the police got to the door grandma said that she didn't know who the people were but they were looking for a guy by the name of Roger, he used to live there, she went on to say that the people didn't believe her that he wasn't there and that they were trying to push up in the house and that she was there alone with us kids. She told us to go in the house as she talked to the police, round bout that time daddy pulled up he jumped out of the car screaming Ms, Millie what's going on where is Trina?, the police pulled their guns on daddy and told him to freeze, grandma who was trying to be a nice old lady for the benefit of the police says oh that's my son in-law, he is asking about his daughter, the police put away their guns and asked daddy what was going on, daddy said I don't know, I was just coming to see my daughter, they let him in the house, when I saw him I ran to him crying I told him all about it, he stays with me until the police leave he says to grandma is it gonna be ok to leave her here tonight? grandma says ain't nobody gonna bother her, you started all of this mess anyway running round there taking that bike, daddy just sat there, he felt bad because he did start that mess but he only just wanted to get my bike back, he says baby stay here, I'll be right back. He goes around to Lil Tony's house, it's dark it looks like no one is home, he takes a deep breath and goes up to the door and knocks, but no one answers as he was walking back to the car Tony's mama comes out and said what's up he says I just came to give you your money back, I didn't mean to cause this much of a problem, my daughter lives there and I don't want her to get hurt, if I give you your money back would you let it go? She said that's all I wanted, daddy gave her a fifty-dollar bill, and said its done right?, she is stuffing the money in her bra and said as long as they don't come around here, daddy said I just don't want y'all going around there, she said ok, daddy started walking to his car she said, you know, you alright, we need mo daddy's like you, daddy didn't say anything he just got back in his car and pulled off. When he got back to grandma's house he knocked on the door and called her name, Ms. Millie. grandma said go open that door, daddy came in and said I went around there and paid them their money back so it's over now, tell your boys to let it go, please. Grandma just stood there, she didn't answer, daddy said Trina come on out here and get your bag lunch, he had made two ham & cheese sandwiches, he had two pops wrapped up in aluminum foil, a small baggy of Doritos, and some lemon cookies, he had it neatly down in a brown paper bag with my name written on it, I was smiling from ear to ear, that was going to be a great lunch, I said thank you, daddy, as I hugged him around his legs, he said daddy don't have any more money well not enough I'm gonna meet you in the morning to give you some spending money, I said ok, daddy said I'm gonna leave now there should be no more trouble if anything happens to call me, I said daddy I was trying to call you but I kept dialing the wrong number, daddy said don't you know my number I said yes I do, he said what is it? and I recited the number, he said awe baby come here and he picks me up he said you were just nervous, he said daddy is so sorry, and I'm gonna make it up to you, daddy looked he could use a hug now so I hugged his neck real tight and I said it's gonna be alright daddy. He says yes it is, he walked me back up the stairs and into the house, he says Ms., Millie I brought her a bag lunch for the field trip tomorrow and ill stop by the school in the morning with her a few dollars for spending, grandma say ok, daddy gives me one more hug he whispers in my ear his phone number real slow he says if something happens and you get scared just close your eyes and take a deep breath and listen for daddy's voice you will hear me say my phone number and you dial it just like daddy said it to you ok, I say ok and he kisses me on the forehead says goodbye to everyone and leaves, grandma says put that bag in the fridge and y'all go to bed.

CHAPTER 32

She Had Enough

I really didn't sleep much that night don't know if it was because I was afraid of the people coming back or the excitement of going on a field trip, either way I tossed and turned all night, when Morning finally came I got up and I asked my grandma if I could wear the new clothes that I had worn home from daddy's house the other day, she just sat there and looked at me like I was crazy, I guess that she was in one of her moods where she wanted to slap me around, but she knew that she couldn't so I just walked away and put the clothes anyway, grandma was making rice and toast, I opened the refrigerator and I didn't see my lunch bag, it wasn't like I had to move anything around because nothing was in there, nothing, not even my lunch bag, I just stood there with the door open, I felt like my little heart just melted and ran down my tummy, down my legs and ended in a puddle on the floor, grandma said close that damn door, I turn around a fired back my damn lunch bag is gone, she yelled what did you say, I said it again my DAMN lunch bag is gone, and as if all of my fear left with my heart, I said I hate it here cant never have nothing, y'all make me sick as I slammed the refrigerator door, grandma didn't miss the opportunity to swing on me, but today I wasn't having non of that, I blocked her hit with my arm and I said don't HIT me no more, grandma threw her head back and said who do you think that your talking too, I screamed I'm talking to you and we both were standing there staring each other down, by that time one of the goons the younger one comes out of the back room and he puts his finger in my face and he says little girl you better calm down I don't know who you think your talking too, I said or what? And I'm talking to her, taking everybody by surprise, he was at a loss for words also as he stood there and so did I, I wasn't even thinking about what they could have done to me, I wasn't scared at that point, she had already done just about everything imaginable so what now, he says as he is walking away mama you better get this little girl, I stand there grandma said you ain't bad standing up there with your wide nose ass looking as ugly as you wanna be and I fired back and what are you looking like, a old skinny dried up witch and your ugly too with your nasty, stankin butt, the goon ran back out of the room and grabbed my arm, I said get your hands off of me, every last one of y'all are going to jail today hit me, go ahead and hit me in my nose again, you coward both of y'all are just bullies always hitting on a little girl, and I snatched my arm from him and walked away, I went into the closet where I sat until I heard the Flintstones introduction song come on, I came out of the closet, no one is saying anything to me, I'm sure that there were just as shocked as I was, I grabbed my back pack and proceeded to walk out the door when grandma said I'm gonna walk y'all to school today, Trina got you a lunch she is holding a cooler that looked like it hadn't been washed since it was found in somebody's trash, I just look her up and down and she opens it, it has a can of Vienna sausage and a pack of saltine crackers, and a thick cut of government cheese that she wrapped up in the bread bag, I look at her again and walk away. On the walk to school, she was trying to make small talk, I had nothing to say, when we got to the school, she handed me the cooler I walk inside the building, and each class had to line up in their classroom number that was marked on the floor, all the other kids either have lunch boxes or brown bags, I'm the only one with a cooler I was so embarrassed, I just stood there as they teased me, once I got up to the classroom Mrs., Frasier had promised my dad that she would look out for me, she says Katrina Honey what's wrong, I didn't say anything she took the cooler from me and she opened it, she said oh my as she slid it under her desk, she said have a seat Katrina, the kids were still laughing and teasing me. Mrs. Frasier said quiet down and take your seats the very next person that says something will not be going on this field trip are we clear, the classroom became silent. She went on to give us the rules for the trip when Then I saw my dad, he was knocking on the classroom door, Mrs. Frasier got up to go to the door she said get out your reading books and read I don't want to hear anyone's mouth or you will not be going to the field trip, as she opens the door and goes out to the hallway to speak to my dad. She says Mr. Sprawls I haven't had the chance to speak to Katrina, what happened why are you here, Daddy said what do you mean what happened? I was just coming to bring her some money to have for spending for the trip, Mrs. Frasier said well something obviously happened because I've never seen her look like this, then she brought this dirty cooler with a pack of crackers, a big block of cheese and a can of Vienna sausage to take for lunch, Daddy says no I made her a lunch myself and brought it to her last night as his nostrils were flaring, he said let me talk to her, Mrs. Frasier walked into the classroom got the cooler and called me into the hallway, daddy was kneeling down to be on my level he said, baby girl what happened, as soon as I saw him the tears started to fall and I tucked my head into his chest and I cried for a few minutes as he was patting my back, he said tell daddy what happened, I said somebody took my lunch and grandma tried to slap me and I blocked her and she cursed at me and I cursed back at her daddy looked at me with wide eyes I swear, I saw his eyes dancing in happiness, then I said then one of her goons grabbed my arm and I told him that they were gonna go to jail if they hit me today, he said oh my God baby, daddy is so sorry he looked in the cooler and said what in the hell is this shit, then he looked up to apologize to Mrs. Frasier who was crying he got up and said I'm sorry, she says no, no its ok. Daddy said what time are you all leaving? Mrs. Frasier said 9:30 daddy said I'll be back I'm going to get her a lunch, he said baby girl stop crying daddy is gonna get you lunch, go blow your nose and clean your face I said ok, as I walked to the bathroom, he told Mrs. Frasier that he would be back he left. Daddy came back on time he had gone somewhere to get me a sandwich it was a grownup sandwich because it had lots of meat not like the ones that we make at home, he had a big bag of Doritos and a pack of cookies, and two grape soda pop, he gave me $20 for spending, thank god that daddy came to save the day. My day started bad but ended up pretty good, I had a good time on the trip and the kids didn't tease me anymore about that dirty cooler. When I got home that afternoon I saw the dirty cooler sitting on the kitchen table I wonder how it had gotten back there. Maybe daddy had taken it back, it was never spoken of again.

CHAPTER 33

Going Home
With Daddy

There was a knock on the door, grandma went to the door, it was my nice Grandma, she said I came to pick up Trina, I said grandma went out to hug her, I said where is daddy she said I told him to stay home that I would pick you up, my mean grandma says, ok come on in, I'll get her things before my nice grandma could answer all we heard was my dad's voice shouting she doesn't need that shit, come on Trina, my nice grandma turned around and said David didn't I tell you to stay at home, Daddy answered yes mama but I couldn't all the stuff that this woman has put me and my baby thru over these past 3 years I just wanted to see her face. My Mean grandma stood there with a smirk on her face "she said you don't want this girl all you want is her check, Daddy shouted back at her you can keep the damn check that's why you were trying to hold on to her you money hungry Bitch, by this time my nice grandma is yelling at him, telling him to get back in his car, one of grandma goons are at the door now he and my dad are arguing back and forth, I don't know who said what but something was said because both my grandmas were arguing and daddy said come on mama off of this porch because I'll catch a case if any one of these Mother fuckers put their hands on you, they continued to argue as we walked down the stairs, daddy said Trina get in the Car, Mama get in your truck and we all drove away. Driving away from that house I felt like I was finally free I was happy, so very happy.

My first night at daddy's house was great, he showed me my room, I had a room, my own bed, I had toys, clothes and shoes, it was great just him and I, He cooked dinner and we talked, it was then when I start telling him about some of the things that happened to me, at my mean grandma's house, he looked sad and said why didn't you tell me, I said that I was afraid too, he hugged me tight and said I don't have to talk about it or think about it anymore. After dinner daddy said, God bless the cook and God bless the dishwasher, we both laughed, I knew for sure that my dishwashing days were over, boy was I wrong, daddy helped me that night and showed me how he liked things done, he says in this house one cooks and the other washes dishes, I said I'll be sure to remember that. After all the cleaning was done we went to bed. During the night I was scared,I was a new place, it was too quiet not like at grandma's where there is always something going on, I went to my dad's room he wasn't there, I was really scared then, so I decided to go in the closet in my bedroom it didn't feel the same as my closet at my grandma's house, I didn't want to be at my grandma's house but I didn't want to be alone either, it was a long night and I didn't get much sleep, I dreamt about this night for so long, but it was nothing like I dreamt.

The next day I told daddy that I was scared and that I was looking for him, he said that he was sorry that he had to bend a few corners, wasn't sure what that meant but he always said it, he asked me if I would like to get a dog, I said yes, after a few days and nights at daddy's house I was getting used to being there alone, I knew that when the weekend came I would be dropped off at my nice grandma's house and I would have my cousins to play with.

At my nice grandma's house, things were different, she had a nice place, and nice furniture there wasn't a bunch of people there, there was always food, and it was nice and quiet. We had to use the back door because she didn't want us in her living room, she had antique furniture, drapes, and carpet it was nice, so everyone congregated in the kitchen.

This particular weekend, I was at my nice grandma's house, all of her kids had grown up left the house except for one, she was the youngest child that my grandma had but she was only 5 years older than I was, I didn't understand having an Aunt so young but I didn't care. I'm sitting at the table with my nice grandma she is talking with me, I'm telling her things that happened at my mean grandma's house, and she calls my young aunt into the kitchen to make Kool-Aid, she and I had always gotten along but since I moved in with my dad she was different towards me. She was making the Kool-Aid and singing this song, 'go back where you came from, nobody wants you here, those were the only lyrics to the song, she sang that about three times before my grandma yelled at her to cut it out and to go to her room, grandma said Trina do you know how to make Kool-Aid, I said yes so I started stirring the kool-aid I took the spoon out to taste it and my young aunt screamed I don't even want any of that Kool-Aid now, my grandma yelled at her again to go to her room. When she left I said why is she mad at me grandma, my grandma said that she is used to being the baby around here she thinks that you're going to take her place I said oh ok, I felt sad that she would be mean to me, I thought for sure that I would be ok over here. I just felt like I didn't belong anywhere. I didn't want to take anybody's place I just wanted to be safe and loved and treated like I mattered to someone, I was mentally and physically drained from everything that I had gone thru, and I didn't want any trouble. I just wished that my dad would come back to get me, I'd rather be alone than feel like I was in the way.

Later that night, grandma says your aunt is still mad and she doesn't want to share her room, she said it's not enough room in the bed with me and grandpa so, grandma is gonna make you a nice place to sleep on the couch ok, I said that's ok grandma I can sleep on the couch, she made the couch for me and I laid down to go to sleep before I went to sleep I talked with Jesus, I said thank you, Jesus, for getting me out of there and I told him to tell mama and queenie that I was ok, I said Jesus I don't want to be in the way here, I don't want to make anybody mad, just stay with me so that I won't be scared at daddy's house I don't care if I have to be alone as long as you can stay with me.

I fell asleep and suddenly I felt someone hit me in the head, I opened my eyes and sat up my eyes were burning bad I couldn't see and I started crying and calling for my grandma, she and my grandpa ran out of their bedroom to take care of it, once she stopped the burning it was found out that someone had poured salt on my eyes lids and hit me in the head, I opened my eyes and the salt fell inside of my eyes, in my mind, I thought here we go again, as we all stood there no one said a word.

I thought that I would be safe here, but WOULD I?

 The End